The Cay

Theodore Taylor was born in North Carolina, in America. He began his writing career aged thirteen compiling sports copy for a Sunday paper. He fell in love with the Caribbean on his first trip there on a petrol tanker in 1943 and his love of this tropical sea is reflected in five of his books, the best known of which is the *The Cay*. The idea for *The Cay*, his first novel for children, came when he was researching an adult book about German submarine attacks in the Second World War. *The Cay* was published in 1969 and it has won eleven literary awards. More recently he has written *Timothy of the Cay*, a prequel-sequel to *The Cay*. Theodore Taylor is married with three children and lives in Laguna Beach, California.

Once you have finished reading *The Cay*, you may be interested in reading the Afterword by Stephanie Nettell on page 119.

THEODORE TAYLOR

The Cay

ILLUSTRATED BY KENNY McKENDRY

PUFFIN BOOKS

PUFFIN BOOKS

Published by the Penguin Group
Penguin Books Ltd, 80 Strand, London WC2R 0RL, England
Penguin Putnam Inc., 375 Hudson Street, New York, New York 10014, USA
Penguin Books Australia Ltd, 250 Camberwell Road, Camberwell, Victoria 3124, Australia
Penguin Books Canada Ltd, 10 Alcorn Avenue, Toronto, Ontario, Canada M4V 3B2
Penguin Books India (P) Ltd, 11 Community Centre, Panchsheel Park, New Delhi – 110 017, India
Penguin Books (NZ) Ltd, Cnr Rosedale and Airborne Roads, Albany, Auckland, New Zealand
Penguin Books (South Africa) (Pty) Ltd, 24 Sturdee Avenue, Rosebank 2196, South Africa

Penguin Books Ltd, Registered Offices: 80 Strand, London WC2R 0RL, England

www.penguin.com

First published in the United States 1969
First published in Great Britain by The Bodley Head 1970
Published in Puffin Books 1973
Published in this edition 1994
25

Text copyright © Theodore Taylor, 1969
Illustrations copyright © Kenny McKendry, 1994
Afterword copyright © Stephanie Nettell, 1994
All rights reserved

Filmset by Datix International Limited, Bungay, Suffolk
Set in 12/15 pt Monophoto Bembo
Printed in England by Clays Ltd, St Ives plc

ISBN-13: 978-0-14-036620-4

*To Dr King's dream, which
can only come true if the
very young know and understand.*

APRIL 1968
LAGUNA BEACH
CALIFORNIA

*L*ike silent, hungry sharks, that swim in the darkness of the sea, the German submarines arrived in the middle of the night.

I was asleep on the second floor of our narrow, gabled green house in Willemstad, on the island of Curaçao, the largest of the Dutch islands just off the coast of Venezuela. I remember that on that moonless night in February 1942 they attacked the big Lago oil refinery on Aruba, the sister island west of us. Then they blew up six of our small lake tankers, the tubby ones that still bring crude oil from Lake Maracaibo to the refinery, Curaçaosche Petroleum Maatschappij, to be made into petrol, paraffin, and diesel oil. One German sub was even sighted off Willemstad at dawn.

So when I woke up there was much excitement in the city, which looks like a part of old Holland, except that all the houses are painted in soft colours, pinks and greens and blues, and there are no dykes.

It was very hard to finish my breakfast because I wanted to go to Punda, the business district, the oldest part of town, and then to Fort Amsterdam where I could look out to sea. If there was an enemy U-boat out there, I wanted to see it and join the people in shaking a fist at it.

I was not frightened, just terribly excited. War was something I'd heard a lot about, but had never seen. The whole world was at war, and now it had come to us in the warm, blue Caribbean.

The first thing that my mother said was, 'Phillip, the enemy has finally attacked the island, and there will be no school today. But you must stay near home. Do you understand?'

I nodded, but I couldn't imagine that a shell from an enemy submarine would pick me out from all the buildings, or hit me if I was standing on the famous pontoon bridge or among the ships way back in the Schottegat or along St Anna Bay.

So later in the morning, when she was busy making sure that all our blackout curtains were in place, and filling extra pots with fresh water, and checking our food supply, I stole away down to the old fort with Henrik van Boven, my Dutch friend who was also eleven.

I had played there many times with Henrik and

other boys when we were a few years younger, imagining we were defending Willemstad against pirates or even the British. They once stormed the island, I knew, long ago. Or sometimes we'd pretend we were the Dutch going out on raids against Spanish galleons. That had happened too. It was all so real that sometimes we could see the tall masted ships coming over the horizon.

Of course, they were only the tattered-sailed native schooners from Venezuela, Aruba, or Bonaire coming in with bananas, oranges, papayas, melons, and vegetables. But to us, they were always pirates, and we'd shout to the noisy black men aboard them. They'd laugh back and go, 'Pow, pow, pow!'

The fort looks as though it came out of a storybook, with gun ports along the high wall that faces the sea. For years, it guarded Willemstad. But this one morning, it did not look like a storybook fort at all. There were real soldiers with rifles and we saw machine guns. Men with binoculars had them trained towards the whitecaps, and everyone was tense. They chased us away, telling us to go home.

Instead, we went down to the Koningin Emma Brug, the famous Queen Emma pontoon bridge, which spans the channel that leads to the huge harbour, the Schottegat. The bridge is built on floats so that it can swing open as ships pass in or out, and it connects Punda with Otrabanda, which means 'other side', the other part of the city.

The view from there wasn't as good as from the fort, but curious people were there, too, just looking. Strangely, no ships were moving in the channel. The *veerboots*, the ferry boats that shuttled cars and people back and forth when the bridge was swung open, were tied up and empty. Even the native schooners were quiet against the docks inside the channel. And the black men were not laughing and shouting the way they usually did.

Henrik said, 'My father told me there is nothing left of Aruba. They hit Sint Nicolaas, you know.'

'Every lake tanker was sunk,' I said.

I didn't know if that were true or not, but Henrik had an irritating way of sounding official since his father was connected with the government.

His face was round and he was chubby. His hair was straw-coloured and his cheeks were always red. Henrik was very serious about everything he said or did. He looked towards Fort Amsterdam.

He said, 'I bet they put big guns up there now.'

That was a safe bet.

And I said, 'It won't be long until the Navy is here.'

Henrik looked at me. 'Our Navy?' He meant the Netherlands Navy.

'No,' I said. 'Ours.' Meaning the American Navy, of course. His little Navy was scattered all over after the Germans took Holland.

Henrik said quietly, 'Our Navy will come too,' and I didn't want to argue with him. Everyone felt bad that Holland had been conquered by the Nazis.

Then an army officer climbed out of a truck and told us all to leave the Queen Emma bridge. He was very stern. He growled, 'Don't you know they could shoot a torpedo up here and kill you all?'

I looked out towards the sea again. It was blue and peaceful, and a good breeze churned it up, making lines of white-caps. White clouds drifted slowly over it. But I couldn't see the usual parade of ships coming towards the harbour; the stubby ones or the massive ones with flags of many nations that steamed slowly up the bay to the Schottegat to load petrol and oil.

The sea was empty; there was not even a sail on it. We suddenly became frightened and ran home to the Scharloo section where we lived.

I guess my face was pale when I went into the house because my mother, who was in the kitchen, asked immediately, 'Where have you been?'

'Punda,' I admitted. 'I went with Henrik.'

My mother got very upset. She grabbed my shoulder and shook it. 'I told you not to go there, Phillip,' she said angrily. 'We are at war! Don't you understand?'

'We just wanted to see the submarines,' I said.

My mother closed her eyes and pulled me up against her thin body. She was like that. One minute, shaking me; the next, holding me.

The radio was on, and a voice said that fifty-six men had died on the lake tankers that were blown up and that the governor of the Netherlands' West Indies had appealed to Washington for help. There was no use in asking Amsterdam. I listened to the sorrowful sound of his voice until my mother's hand switched it to off.

Finally she said, 'You'll be safe if you do what we tell you to do. Don't leave the garden again today.'

She seemed very nervous. But then she was often

nervous. My mother was always afraid I'd fall off the sea wall, or tumble out of a tree, or cut myself with a pocketknife. Henrik's mother wasn't that way. She laughed a lot and said, 'Boys, boys, boys.'

Late in the afternoon, my father, whose name was also Phillip – Phillip Enright – returned home from the refinery where he was working on the programme to increase production of aviation fuel. He'd been up since two o'clock, my mother said, and please don't ask him too many questions.

They had phoned him that morning to say that the Germans might attempt to shell the refinery and the oil storage tanks, and that he must report to help fight the fires. I had never seen him so tired, and I didn't ask as many questions as I wanted to.

Until the past year, my father and I had done a lot of things together. Fishing or sailing our small boat, or taking long hikes around Krup Bay or Seroe Male, or just going out into the *koenoekoe*, the countryside, together. He knew a lot about trees and fish and birds. But now he always seemed busy. Even on a Sunday, he'd shake his head and say, 'I'm sorry, guy, I have to work.'

After he had had his pint of cold Dutch ale (he had one every night in the living room after he came home), I asked, 'Will they shoot at us tonight?'

He looked at me gravely and answered, 'I don't know, Phillip. They might. I want you and your mother to sleep down here tonight, not on the first floor. I don't think you're in any danger, but it's better to sleep down here.'

'How many of them are out there?' I thought they might be like schools of fish. Dozens, maybe. I wanted to be able to tell Henrik exactly what my father knew about the submarines.

He shook his head. 'No one knows, Phillip. But there must be three of them around the islands. The attacks were in three different places.'

'They came all the way from Germany?'

He nodded. 'Or from bases in France,' he said, loading his pipe.

'Why can't we go out and fight them?' I asked.

My father laughed sadly and tapped his long forefinger on my chest. 'You'd like that, would you? But we have nothing to fight them with, son. We can't go out in motorboats and attack them with rifles.'

My mother came in from the kitchen to say, 'Stop asking so many silly questions, Phillip. I told you not to do that.'

Father looked at her strangely. He had always answered my questions. 'He has a right to know. He's involved here, Grace.'

My mother looked back at him. 'Yes, unfortunately,' she said.

My mother, I knew, had not wanted to come to Curaçao in late 1939, but my father had argued that he was needed for the war effort even though the United States was not at war then. Royal Dutch Shell had borrowed him from his American company because he was an expert in refineries and petrol production. But the moment she saw it, my mother decided she didn't like Curaçao and she often complained about the smell of petrol and oil whenever the trade winds died down.

It was very different in Virginia where my father had been in charge of building a new refinery on the banks of the Elizabeth River. We'd lived in a small white house on an acre of land with many trees. My mother often talked about the house and the trees; about the change of seasons and the friends she had there. She said it was nice and safe in Virginia.

My father would answer quietly, 'There's no place nice and safe right now.'

I remembered the summers with lightning bugs and honeysuckle smells; the cold winters when the fields would all be brown and would crackle under my feet. I didn't remember too much else. I was only seven when we'd moved to the Caribbean.

I guess my mother was homesick for Virginia, where no one talked Dutch, and there was no smell of petrol or oil, and there weren't as many black people around.

Now, there was a cold silence between my mother and my father. Lately, it had been happening more and more often. She went back into the kitchen.

I said to him, 'Why can't they use aircraft and bomb the submarines?'

He was staring towards the kitchen and didn't hear me. I repeated it.

He sighed. 'Oh yes. Same answer, Phillip. There are no fighting aircraft down here. To tell you the truth, we don't have any weapons.'

We finished dinner just as it was getting dark, and my father went outside to look at our house. He wanted to see if the blackout curtains were working. While my mother and I stood by each window, he called out if he saw the slightest crack of light. By the governor's orders, not a light could shine anywhere on the whole island, he said. Then he went back to the refinery.

I crawled on to the couch downstairs about nine o'clock but I couldn't sleep. I kept thinking about the U-boats off our coast and those lake tankers with barefooted Chinese sailors on board. I guess I was waiting for the U-boats to send a shell towards Willemstad.

Then I began to wonder if the Germans would send soldiers too. About nine-thirty I sneaked out of bed, went to the tool house, and took a hatchet out. I put it under the couch. It was the only thing I could think of to use for fighting the Germans.

It must have been eleven o'clock when my father returned from the refinery to get all the flashlights we had in the house. They talked in low voices, but I could hear them.

Mother said, 'It's too dangerous to stay here now.'

My father answered, 'Grace, you know I can't leave.'

She said, 'Well, then Phillip and I must go back. We'll go back to Norfolk and wait until the danger is over.'

I sat up in bed, unable to believe what I was hearing, My father said, 'There's more danger in the trip back, unless you go by air, than there is in staying here. If they do shell us, they won't hit Scharloo.'

Mother said sharply, 'You know I won't fly. I'd be frightened to death to fly.'

'We'll talk about it later.' My father sounded miserable. Soon afterwards he returned to the refinery again.

I thought about leaving the island, and it saddened me. I loved the old fort, and the schooners, the Ruyterkade market with the noisy chickens and squealing pigs, the black people shouting; I loved the koenoekoe with its giant cactus; the divi-divi trees, their odd branches all on the leeward side of the trunk; the beautiful sandy beach at West-punt. And I'd miss Henrik van Boven.

I also knew that Henrik and his mother would think us cowardly if we left just because a few German submarines were off Curaçao. I was awake most of the night.

The next morning my father said that the Chinese crews on the lake tankers that shuttled crude oil across the sand bars at Maracaibo had refused to sail without naval escorts. He said the refinery would have to close down within a day, and that meant precious petrol and oil could not go to England, or to General Montgomery in the African desert.

For seven days, not a ship moved by the Queen Emma bridge, and there was gloom over Willemstad. The people had been very proud that the little islands of Aruba and Curaçao were now among the most important islands in the world; that victory or defeat depended on them. They were angry with the Chinese crews, and on the third day, my father said that mutiny charges had been placed against them.

'But,' he said, 'you must understand they are very frightened, and some of the people who are angry with them would not sail the little ships either.'

He explained to me what it must feel like to ride the cargoes of crude oil, knowing that a torpedo or shell could turn the whole ship into flames any moment. Even though he wasn't a sailor, he volunteered to help man the lake tankers.

Soon, of course, we might also run out of fresh water. It rains very little in the Dutch West Indies unless there is a hurricane, and water from the few wells has a heavy salt content. The big tankers from the United States or England always carried fresh water to use in ballast, and then it was distilled again so that we could drink it. But now, all the big tankers were being held up in their ports until the submarines could be chased away.

Towards the end of the week, we began to run out of fresh vegetables because the schooner-men were also afraid. Now, my mother talked constantly about the submarines, the lack of water, and the shortage of food. It almost seemed that she was using the war as an excuse to leave Curaçao.

'The ships will be moving again soon,' my father said confidently, and he was right.

I think it was 21 February that some of the Chinese sailors agreed to sail to Lake Maracaibo. But on that same day a Norwegian tanker, headed for Willemstad, was torpedoed off Curaçao, and fear again swept over the old city. Without our ships, we were helpless.

Then a day or two later, my father took me into the Schottegat where they were completing the loading of the S.S. *Empire Tern*, a big British tanker. She had machine guns fore and aft, one of the few armed ships in the harbour.

Although the trade wind was blowing, the smell of petrol and oil lay heavy over the Schottegat. Other empty tankers were there, high out of the water, awaiting orders to sail once they had cargoes. The men on them were leaning over the rail watching all the activity on the *Empire Tern*.

I looked on as the thick hoses that were attached to her quivered when the petrol was pumped into her tanks. The fumes shimmered in the air, and one by one, they 'topped' her tanks, loading them right to the brim and securing them for sea. No one said very much. With all that aviation fuel around, it was dangerous.

Then in the afternoon, we went to Punda and stood near the pontoon bridge as she steamed slowly down St Anna Bay. Many others had come to watch, too, even the governor, and we all cheered as she passed, setting out on her lonely voyage to England. There, she would help refuel the Royal Air Force.

The sailors on the *Empire Tern*, which was painted a dull white but had rust streaks all over her, waved back at us and held up their fingers in a V-for-victory sign.

We watched until the pilot boat, having picked up the harbour pilot from the *Empire Tern*, began to race back to Willemstad. Just as we were ready to go, there was an explosion and we looked towards the sea. The *Empire Tern* had vanished in a wall of red flames, and black smoke was beginning to boil into the sky.

Someone screamed, 'There it is.' We looked off to one side of the flames, about a mile away, and saw a black shape in the water, very low. It was a German submarine, surfaced now to watch the ship die.

A tug and several small motorboats headed out

towards the *Tern*, but it was useless. Some of the women cried at the sight of her, and I saw men, my father included, with tears in their eyes. It didn't seem possible that only a few hours before I had been standing on her deck. I was no longer excited about the war; I had begun to understand that it meant death and destruction.

The same night, my mother told my father, 'I'm taking Phillip back to Norfolk.' I knew she'd made up her mind.

He was tired and disheartened over what had happened to the *Empire Tern*. He did not say much. But I do remember him saying, 'Grace, I think you are making a mistake. You are both quite safe here in Scharloo.' I wondered why he didn't simply order her to stay. But he wasn't that kind of a man.

The sunny days and dark, still nights passed slowly during March. The ships had begun to sail again, defying the submarines. Some were lost. Henrik and I often went down to Punda to watch them go out, hoping that they would be safe.

Neither my father nor my mother talked very much about us leaving. I thought that when two American destroyers arrived, along with the Dutch cruiser *Van Kingsbergen*, to protect the lake tankers, Mother would change her mind. But it only made her more nervous.

Then one day in early April, she said, 'Your father has finally secured passage for us, so today will be your last day in school here, Phillip. We'll start packing tomorrow, and on Friday, we leave aboard a ship for Miami. Then we'll take the train to Norfolk.'

Suddenly, I felt hollow inside. Then I became angry and accused her of being a coward. She told me to go off to school. I said I hated her.

All that day in school, I tried to think of what I could do. I thought about going somewhere and hiding until the ship had sailed, but on an island the size of Curaçao, there is no place to hide Also, I knew it would cause my father trouble.

That night when he got home, I told him I wanted to stay with him. He smiled and put his long, thin arm around my shoulder. He said, 'No, Phillip, I think it is best that you go with your mother. At a time like this, I can't be at home very much.'

His voice seemed sad, although he was trying to be cheerful. He told me how wonderful it would be to return to the United States; how many things I had missed while we were on the island. I couldn't think of one.

Then I talked to my mother about staying on in Willemstad, and she became very upset with both of us. She said that we didn't love her and began to cry.

My father finally ended it by saying, 'Phillip, the decision is made. You'll leave Friday with your mother.'

So I packed, with her help, and said good-bye to Henrik van Boven and the other boys. I told them we'd be gone just a short time; that we were going to visit my grandparents, my mother's parents, in Norfolk.

But I had the feeling that it might be a very long time before I saw Curaçao and my father again.

Early Friday morning, we boarded the S.S. *Hato* in St Anna Channel. She was a small Dutch freighter with a high bow and stern, and a bridge house in the middle between two well decks. I had seen her often in St Anna Bay. Usually, she ran between Willemstad, Aruba, and Panama. She had a long stack and always puffed thick, black smoke.

In our cabin, which was on the starboard side and opened out to the boat deck, my father said, 'Well, you can rest easy, Phillip. The Germans would never waste a torpedo on this old tub.' Yet I saw him looking over the lifeboats. Then he inspected the fire hoses on the boat deck. I knew he was worried.

There were eight other passengers aboard, and they were all saying good-bye to their relatives just as we were saying good-bye to my father. In the tradition, people brought flowers and wine. It was almost like sailing in the days before the war, they told me.

Father was smiling and very gay but when the *Hato*'s whistle blasted out three times, meaning it was time to go, he said good-bye to us between clenched teeth. I clung to him for a long time. Finally, he said, 'Take good care of your mother.'

I said I would.

We sailed down St Anna Bay, and the Queen Emma bridge parted for us. Through watery eyes, I saw the fort and the old buildings of Punda and Otrabanda. Native schooners were beating in from the sea.

Then my mother pointed. I saw a tall man standing on the wall of Fort Amsterdam, waving at us. I knew it was my father. I'll never forget that tall, lonely figure standing on the sea wall.

The S.S. *Hato* took her first bite of open sea and began to pitch gently. We turned towards Panama, as we had to make a call there before proceeding to Miami. Down on the well decks, fore and aft, were four massive pumps that had to be delivered to Colón, the port at the Atlantic entrance to the Panama Canal.

I stayed out on deck for a long time, sitting by the lifeboat, looking back at Curaçao, feeling lonely and sad.

Finally my mother said, 'Come inside now.'

CHAPTER 3

We were torpedoed at about three o'clock in the morning on 6 April 1942, two days after leaving Panama.

I was thrown from the top bunk and suddenly found myself on my hands and knees on the deck. We could hear the ship's whistle blowing constantly, and there were sounds of metal wrenching and much shouting. The whole ship was shuddering. It felt as though we'd stopped and were dead in the water.

My mother was very calm, not at all like she was at home. She talked quietly while she got dressed, telling me to tie my shoes, and be certain to carry my wool

18

sweater, and to put on my leather jacket. Her hands were not shaking.

She helped me put on my life jacket, then put hers on, saying, 'Now, remember everything that we were told about abandoning ship.' The officers had held drills every day.

As she was speaking, there was another violent explosion. We were thrown against the cabin door, which the steward had warned us not to lock because it might become jammed. We pushed it open and went out to the boat deck, which was already beginning to tilt.

Everything was bright red, and there were great crackling noises. The entire afterpart of the ship was on fire, and sailors were launching the lifeboat that was on our deck. Steam lines had broken, and the steam was hissing out. Heat from the fire washed over us.

When the lifeboat had been swung out, the captain came down from the bridge. He was a small, wiry white-haired man and was acting the way I'd been told captains should act. He stood by the lifeboat in the fire's glow, very alert, giving orders to the crew. He was carrying a briefcase and a navigation instrument I knew to be a sextant. On the other side of the ship, another lifeboat was being launched.

Near us, two sailors with axes chopped at lines, and two big life rafts plunged towards the water, which looked black except for pools of fire from burning fuel oil.

The captain shouted, 'Get a move on! Passengers into the boats!' Tins of lubricating oil in the afterholds had ignited and were exploding, but the ones forward had not been exposed to the fire.

A sailor grabbed my mother's hand and helped her in, and then I felt myself being passed into the hands of a sailor on the boat. The other passengers were helped in, and someone yelled, 'Lower away.' At that moment, the *Hato* lurched heavily and something happened to the boat falls.

The bow tilted downwards, and the next thing I knew we were all in the water. I saw my mother near me and yelled to her. Then something hit me from above.

A long time later (four hours I was told), I opened my eyes to see blue sky above. It moved back and forth, and I could hear the slap of water. I had a terrible pain in my head. I closed my eyes again, thinking maybe I was dreaming. Then a voice said, 'Young bahss, how are you feelin'?'

I turned my head.

I saw a huge, very old Negro sitting on the raft near me. He was ugly. His nose was flat and his face was broad; his head was a mass of wiry grey hair. For a moment, I could not figure out where I was or who he was. Then I remembered seeing him working with the deck gang of the *Hato*.

I looked around for my mother, but there was no one else on the raft. Just this huge Negro, myself, and a big black and grey cat that was licking his haunches.

The Negro said, 'You 'ad a mos' terrible crack on d'ead, bahss. A strong-back glanc' offen your 'ead, an' I harl you board dis raff.'

He crawled over towards me. His face couldn't have been blacker, or his teeth whiter. They made an alabaster trench in his mouth, and his pink-purple lips peeled over them like the meat of a conch shell. He had a big welt, like a scar, on his left cheek. I knew he was West Indian. I had seen many of them in Willemstad, but he was the biggest one I'd ever seen.

I sat up, asking, 'Where are we? Where is my mother?'

The Negro shook his head with a frown. 'I true believe you mut-thur is safe an' soun' on a raff like dis. Or mebbe dey harl 'er into d'boat. I true believe dat.'

Then he smiled at me, his face becoming less terrifying. 'As to our veree location, I mus' guess we are somewhar roun' d'cays, somewhar mebbe fifteen latitude an' eighty long. We should 'ave pass dem til' dat mos' treacherous torpedo split d'veree hull. Two minute downg, at d'mos'.'

I looked all around us. There was nothing but blue sea with occasional patches of orange-brown seaweed. No sight of the *Hato*, or other rafts, or boats. Just the sea and a few birds that wheeled over it. That lonely sea, and the sharp pains in my head, and the knowledge that I was here alone with a black man instead of my mother made me break into tears.

Finally the black man said, looking at me from bloodshot eyes, 'Now, young bahss, I mos' feel like dat my own self, Timothy, but 'twould be of no particular use to do dat, eh?' His voice was rich calypso, soft and musical, the words rubbing off like velvet.

I felt a little better, but my head ached fiercely.

He nodded towards the cat. 'Dis is Stew, d'cook's cat. He climb on d'raff, an' I 'ad no heart to trow 'im off.' Stew was still busy licking. ''E got oi-ll all ovah hisself from d'wattah.'

I looked closer at the black man. He was extremely old yet he seemed powerful. Muscles rippled over the ebony of his arms and around his shoulders. His chest was thick and his neck was the size of a small tree trunk. I looked at his hands and feet. The skin was alligatored and cracked, tough from age and walking barefoot on the hot decks of schooners and freighters.

He saw me examining him and said gently, 'Put your 'ead back downg, young bahss, an' rest awhile longer. Do not look direct at d'sun. 'Tis to powerful.'

I felt seasick and crawled to the side to vomit. He came up beside me, holding my head in his great clamshell hands. It didn't matter, at that moment, that he was black and ugly. He murmured, 'Dis be good, dis be good.'

When it was over, he helped me back to the centre of the raft, saying, ''Tis mos' natural for you to do dis. 'Tis d'shock o' havin' all dis mos' terrible ting 'appen.'

I then watched as he used his powerful arms and hands to rip up boards from the outside edges of the raft. He pounded them back together on cleats, forming two triangles; then he jammed the bases into slots between the raft boards. He stripped off his shirt and his pants, then demanded mine. I don't know what happened to my leather jacket or my sweater. But soon, we had a flimsy shelter from the burning sun.

Crawling under it to sprawl beside me, he said, 'We 'ave rare good luck, young bahss. D'wattah kag did not bus' when d'raff was launch, an' we 'ave a few biscuit, some choclade, an' d'matches in d'tin is dry. So we 'ave rare good luck.' He grinned at me then.

I was thinking that our luck wasn't so good. I was thinking about my mother on another boat or raft, not knowing I was all right. I was thinking about my father back in Willemstad. It was terrible not to be able to tell him where I was. He'd have boats and planes out within hours.

I guess the big Negro saw the look on my face. He said, 'Do not be despair, young bahss. Someone will fin' us. Many schooner go by dis way, an' dis also be d'ship track to Jamaica, an' on.'

After a bit, lulled by the bobbing of the raft and by the soft, pleasant sounds of the sea against the oil barrel floats, I went to sleep again. I was very tired and my head still ached. The piece of timber must have struck a glancing blow on the left side.

When I next awakened, it was late afternoon. The sun had edged down and the breeze across us was cool. But I felt very hot and the pain had not gone away. The Negro was sitting with his back towards me, humming something in calypso. His back was a great wall of black flesh, and I saw a cruel scar on one shoulder.

I asked, 'What is your name?'

Hearing my voice, he turned with a wide grin. 'Ah, you are back wit' me. It 'as been lonesome dese veree hours.'

I repeated, 'What is your name?'

'My own self? Timothy!'

'Your last name?'

He laughed, 'I 'ave but one name. 'Tis Timothy.'

'Mine is Phillip Enright, Timothy.' My father had always taught me to address anyone I took to be an adult as 'mister', but Timothy didn't seem to be a mister. Besides, he was black.

He said, 'I knew a Phillip who feesh out of St Jawn, but an outrageous mahn he was.' He laughed deep inside himself.

I asked him for a drink of water.

He nodded agreeably, saying, 'D'sun do parch.' He lifted a hinged section of the raft flooring and drew out the keg, which was about two feet long. There was a tin cup lashed to it. Careful not to spill a drop, he said, ''Tis best to 'ave only an outrageous smahl amount. Jus' enough to wet d'tongue.'

'Why?' I asked. 'That is a large keg.'

He scanned the barren sea and then looked back at me, his old eyes growing remote. 'D'large kag 'ave a way o' losin' its veree size.'

'You said we would be picked up soon,' I reminded him.

'Ah, yes,' he said instantly, 'but we mus' be wise 'bout what we 'ave.'

I drank the tiny amount of water he'd poured out and asked for more. He regarded me silently a moment, then said, his eyes squinting. 'A veree lil' more, young bahss.'

My lips were parched and my throat was dry. I wanted a whole cup. 'Please fill it up,' I said.

Timothy poured only a few drops into the bottom.

'That isn't enough,' I complained. I felt I could drink three cups of it. But he pressed the wooden stopper firmly back into the keg, ignoring me.

I said, 'I must have water, Timothy. I'm very hot.'

Without answering, he opened the trap in the raft and secured the keg again. It was then that I began to learn what a stubborn old man he could be. I began to dislike Timothy.

'Young bahss,' he said, coming back under the shelter, 'mebbe before d'night, a schooner will pass dis way, an' if dat 'appens, you may drink d'whole kag. Mebbe d'schooner will not pass dis way, so we mus' make our wattah last.'

I said defiantly, 'A schooner will find us. And my father has ships out looking for us.'

Without even glancing at me, he answered, 'True, young bahss.' Then he closed his eyes and would not speak to me any more. He just sprawled out, a mound of silent black flesh.

I couldn't hold the tears back. I'm sure he heard me, but he didn't move a muscle of his face. Neither did he look up when I crawled out from under the shelter to get as far away from him as I could. I stayed on the edge of the raft for a long time, thinking about home and rubbing Stew Cat's back.

Although I hadn't thought so before, I was now beginning to believe that my mother was right. She didn't like them. She didn't like it when Henrik and I would go down to St Anna Bay and play near the schooners. But it was always fun. The black people would laugh at us and toss us bananas or papayas.

She'd say, when she knew where we'd been, 'They are not the same as you, Phillip. They are different and they live differently. That's the way it must be.' Henrik, who'd grown up in Curaçao with them, couldn't understand why my mother felt this way.

I yelled over at him, 'You're saving all the water for yourself.'

I don't think he was asleep, but he didn't answer.

When the sky began to turn a deep blue, Timothy roused himself and looked around. He said, with just an unfriendly glance at me, 'If luck be, d'flyin' feesh will flop on d'raff. We can save a few biscuit by eatin' d'feesh. Too, wattah is in d'feesh.'

I was hungry but the thought of eating raw fish didn't appeal to me. I said nothing.

Just before dark, they began skimming across the water, their short, winglike fins taking them on flights of twenty or thirty feet, sometimes more.

A large one shot out of the water, skimmed towards us, and then slammed into the raft flooring. Timothy grabbed it, shouting happily. He rapped its head with his knife handle and tossed it beneath the shelter. Soon another came aboard, not so large. Timothy grabbed it, too.

Before total darkness, he had skinned them, deftly

cutting meat from their sides. He handed me the two largest pieces. 'Eat dem,' he ordered.

I shook my head.

He looked at me in the fading light and said softly, 'We will 'ave no other food tonight. You bes' eat dem, young bahss.' With that, he pressed a piece of the fish against his teeth, sucking at it noisily.

Yes, they were different. They ate raw fish.

I turned away from him, over on my stomach. I thought about Curaçao, warm and safe; about our gabled house in Scharloo, and about my father. Suddenly I blamed my mother because I was on the raft with this stubborn old black man. It was all her fault. She'd wanted to leave the island.

I blurted out, 'I wouldn't even be here with you if it wasn't for my mother.'

I knew Timothy was staring at me through the darkness when he said, 'She started dis terrible wahr, eh, young bahss?' He was a shadowy shape across the raft.

CHAPTER 4

*T*otal darkness blotted out the sea, and it became cold and damp. Timothy took the shelter down, and we both pulled our shirts and pants back on. They were stiff from salt and felt clammy. The wind picked up, blowing fine chill spray across the raft. Then the stars came out.

We stayed in the middle of the raft, side by side, as it drifted aimlessly over the sea. Stew Cat rubbed his back against the bottoms of my feet and then curled down there. I was glad because he was warm.

I was thinking that it was very strange for me, a boy from Virginia, to be lying beside this giant Negro out

28

on the ocean. And I guess maybe Timothy was thinking the same thing.

Once, our bodies touched. We both drew back, but I drew back faster. In Virginia, I knew they'd always lived in their sections of town, and us in ours. A few times, I'd gone down through the shacks of coloured town with my father. They sold spicy crabs in one shack, I remember.

I saw them mostly in the summer, down by the river, fishing or swimming naked, but I didn't really know any of them. And in Willemstad, I didn't know them very well either. Henrik van Boven did, though, and he was much easier with them.

I asked, 'Timothy, where is your home?'

'St Thomas,' he said. 'Charlotte Amalie, on St Thomas.' He added, ''Tis a Virgin Islan'.'

'Then you are American,' I said. I remembered from school that we had bought the Virgins from Denmark.

He laughed. 'I suppose, young bahss. I nevar gave it much thought. I sail all d'islan's, as well as Venezuela, Colombo, Panama ... I jus' nevar gave it much thought I was American.'

I said, 'Your parents were African, Timothy?'

He laughed, low and soft. 'Young bahss, you want me to say I true come from Afre-ca?'

'You say what you want.' It was just that Timothy looked very much like the men I'd seen in the jungle pictures. Flat nose and heavy lips.

He shook his head. 'I 'ave no recollection o' anythin' 'cept dese islan's. 'Tis pure outrageous, but I do not remember anythin' 'bout a place called Afre-ca.'

I didn't know if he was telling the truth or not. He looked pure African. I said. 'What about your mother?'

Now, there was deep laughter in his voice. ''Tis even more outrageous I do not remember a fatha or my mut-thur. I was raise by a woman call Hannah Gumbs . . .'

'Then you are an orphan,' I said.

'I guess, young bahss, I guess.' He was chuckling to himself, rich and deep.

I looked over towards him, but again, he was just a shadowy shape, a large mound. 'How old are you, Timothy?' I asked.

'Dat fact is also veree mysterious. Lil' more dan sixty, 'cause d'muscle in my legs b'speakin' to me, complain all d'time. But to be true, I do not know exact.'

I was amazed that any man shouldn't know his own age. I was almost certain now that Timothy had indeed come from Africa, but I didn't tell him that. I said, 'I'm almost twelve.' I wanted him to know I was almost twelve so that he would stop treating me as though I were half that age.

'Dat is a veree important age,' Timothy agreed. 'Now, you mus' get some natural sleep. Tomorrow might be a veree long day, an' we 'ave much to do.'

I laughed. There we were on that bucking raft with nothing to do except watch for schooners or aircraft. 'What do we have to do?' I asked.

His eyes groped through the darkness for mine. He came up on his elbows. 'Stay alive, young bahss, dat's what we 'ave to do.'

Soon, it became very cold and I began shivering. Part of it was coldness, but there was also fear. If the raft tipped over, sharks would slash at us, I knew.

My head was aching violently again. During the day, the pain had been dull, but now it was shooting along both sides of my head. Once, sometime during the early night I felt his horny hand on my forehead. Then he shifted my body, placing it on the other side of him.

He murmured, 'Young bahss, d'wind 'as shift. You'll be warmer on dis side.'

I was still shivering, and soon he gathered me against him, and Stew Cat came back to be a warm ball against my feet. I could now smell Timothy, tucked up against him. He didn't smell like my father or my mother. Father always smelled of bay rum, the shaving lotion he used, and Mother smelled of some kind of perfume or cologne. Timothy smelled different and strong, like the black men who worked on the decks of the tankers when they were loading. After a while, I didn't mind the smell because Timothy's back was very warm.

The raft plunged on across the light swells throughout the long night.

I do not think he slept much during the night, but I'd been told that old people didn't sleep much anyway. I woke up when there was a pale band of light to the east, and Timothy said, 'You fare well, young bahss? How is d'ead?'

'It still hurts,' I admitted.

Timothy said, 'A crack on d'ead takes a few days to go 'way.' He opened the trap on the raft to pull out the water keg and the tin containing the biscuits, the chocolate squares and dry matches.

I sat up, feeling dizzy. He allowed me half a cup of water and two hard biscuits, then fed Stew Cat with a wedge of leftover flying fish. We ate in silence as the light crept steadily over the smooth, oily sea. The wind had died and already the sun was beginning to scorch.

Timothy chewed slowly on half a biscuit. 'Today, young bahss, a schooner will pass. I'd bet a jum on dat.'

'I hope so,' I said.

'I do tink we are not too far from Providencia an' San Andrés.'

I looked hard at Timothy. 'Are they islands?'

He nodded.

I kept looking at him. It seemed there was a film, a haze, separating us. I rubbed my eyes and opened them again. But the haze was still there. I glanced over at the red ball of sun, now clear of the horizon. It seemed dim. I said, 'I think there is something wrong with my eyes.'

Timothy said, 'I warn you! You look direct at d'sun yestiddy.'

Yes, that was it! I'd looked at the sun too much.

'Today,' Timothy said, 'do not eben look at d'wattah. D'glare is bad too.'

He went about setting up the triangles for our shelter,

and I took off my clothes. After he had draped my pants and shirt, I got under the shelter. The pain in my head was almost unbearable now, and I remember moaning. Timothy tore off a piece of his shirt from the shelter roof, soaked it in fresh water and placed it over my eyes. There was worry in his voice as he talked.

A while later, I took the cloth off my eyes and looked up. The inside of our shelter was shadowy and dark, but the pain had begun to go away. 'It doesn't hurt as much any more,' I said.

'Ah, see, it jus' takes time, young bahss.'

I put the cool cloth back over my eyes and went to sleep again. When I woke up, it was night. Yet the air felt hot, and the breeze that came across the raft was warm. I lay there thinking.

'What time is it?' I asked.

''Bout ten.'

'At night?'

There was puzzlement in his voice. ''Tis day.'

I put my hand in front of my face. Even in the very blackest night, you can see your own hand. But I could not see mine.

I screamed to Timothy, 'I'm blind, I'm blind.'

'What?' His voice was a frightened roar.

Then I knew he was bending over me. I felt his breath in my face. He said, 'Young bahss, you cannot be blin'.' He pulled me roughly from the shelter.

'Look at d'sun,' he ordered. His hands pointed my face. I felt the strong warmth against it, but everything was black.

The silence seemed to last for ever as he held my face towards the sun. Then a long, shuddering sigh came from his great body. He said, very gently, 'Now, young bahss, you mus' lie downg an' rest. What 'as happen will go 'way. 'Tis all natural temporary.' But his voice was hollow.

I got down on the hot boards, blinking my eyes again and again, trying to lift the curtain of blackness. I touched them. They did not feel any different. Then I realized that the pain had gone away. It had gone away but left me blind.

I could hear my voice saying, far off, 'I don't feel any pain, Timothy. The pain has gone away.'

I guess he was trying to think it all out. In a few minutes, he answered, 'Once, ovah 'round Barbados, a mahn 'ad an outrageous crack on d'ead when a sailin' boom shift. Dis mahn was blin' too. Tree whole day 'e saw d'night. Den it true went away.'

'Do you think that is what will happen to me?'

'I tink dat be true, young bahss,' he said.

Then he became very quiet.

After a moment, lying there in darkness, hearing the creak of the raft and feeling its motion, it all hit me. I was blind and we were lost at sea.

I began to crawl, screaming for my mother and my father, but felt his hard hands on my arms. He held me tight and said, low and soft, 'Young bahss, young bahss.' He kept repeating it.

I'll never forget that first hour of knowing I was blind. I was so frightened that it was hard for me to breathe. It was as if I'd been put inside something that was all dark and I couldn't get out.

I remember that at one point my fear turned to anger. Anger at Timothy for not letting me stay in the water with my mother, and anger at her because I was on the raft. I began hitting him and I remember him saying, 'If dat will make you bettah, go 'ead.'

After a while, I felt very tired and fell back on the hot boards.

CHAPTER 5

I guess it was towards noon on the third day aboard the raft that Timothy said tensely, 'I 'ear a motah.'

'A motah?'

'Sssssh.'

I listened. Yes, there was a far-off engine sound coming in faintly above the slap of the sea. Then I could hear Timothy moving around. ''Tis an aircraft,' he said.

My heart began to pound. *They were looking for us.* I felt around, then crawled from beneath the shelter to look towards the sound. But I could see nothing.

I heard the hinges on the trap door creak. Timothy

said quietly, as though afraid to chase the sound away, 'It knowin' what we are doin' 'ere by seein' smoke, I do believe.'

He ripped down one of the triangle legs, and I heard cloth tearing. Soon he said, 'We made d'torch, young bahss. D'mahn up dere be seein' d'smoke all right, all right.'

The faint drone of the aircraft seemed closer now. In a moment, I smelled cloth burning and knew he was holding the wrapped piece of wood towards the sky.

He shouted, 'Look downg 'ere.'

But already the drone seemed to be fading.

Timothy yelled, 'I see it, I see it! Way to port!'

I tried to make my eyes cut through the darkness. 'Is he coming our way?'

'Don' know, don' know, young bahss,' Timothy replied anxiously.

I said, 'I can't hear it now.' There was nothing in the air but the sea sounds.

Timothy shouted, 'Look downg 'ere! Dere is a raff wit a lil' blin' boy, an' old mahn, an' Stew Cat. Look downg 'ere, I tell you.'

The drone could not be heard. Just the slap of the water and the sound of the light wind making our shelter flap.

We were alone again on the ocean.

After a moment of silence, I heard the sizzle of the water as Timothy doused the torch. He sighed deeply, 'I be ready next time for true. Let d'torch dry, den I be ready.'

Soon he sat down beside me. ''Tis a good ting not to harass d'soul ovah dis. We are edgin' into d'aircraft track, same as d'ship dey run.'

I said nothing but put my head down on my knees.

'Do not be dishearten, young bahss. Today, we will be foun', to be true.'

But the long, hot day was passing without sight of anything. I knew Timothy was constantly scanning the sea. It was all so calm now that the raft didn't even seem to be drifting. Once, I crawled over to the edge to touch the warm water and felt Timothy right behind me.

He said, 'Careful, young bahss. D'sharks always hungry, always waitin' for d'mahn to fall ovahboard.'

Drawing back from the edge, I asked, 'Are there many here?'

'Yes, many 'ere. But long as we 'ave our raff, they do not meliss us.'

Standing on the sea wall at Willemstad, sometimes I'd seen their fins in the water. I'd also seen them on the dock at the Ruyterkade market, their mouths open and those sharp teeth grinning.

I went back under the shelter, spending a long time rubbing Stew Cat. He purred and pushed himself along my body. I was glad that I had seen him and had seen Timothy before going blind. I thought how awful it would have been to awaken on the raft and not know what they looked like.

Timothy must have been standing over us, for he said, 'D'cot not good luck.' After a moment he added, 'But to cause d'death of a cot is veree bad luck.'

'I don't think Stew Cat is bad luck,' I said. 'I'm glad he is here with us.'

Timothy did not answer, but turned back, I guess, to watch the sea again. I could imagine those bloodshot eyes, set in that massive, scarred black face, sweeping over the sea.

'Tell me what's out there, Timothy,' I said. It was very important to know that now. I wanted to know everything that was out there.

He laughed. 'Jus' miles o' blue wattah, miles o' blue wattah.'

'Nothing else?'

He realized what I meant. 'Oh, to be sure, young bahss. I see a feesh jump way fo'ward. Dat mean large feesh chase 'im. Den awhile back, a turtle pass us port side, but too far out to reach 'im back . . .'

His eyes were becoming mine. 'What's in the sky, Timothy?'

'In d'sky?' He searched it. 'No clouds, young bahss, jus' blue like 'twas yestiddy. But now an' den, I see a petrel. While ago, a booby . . .'

I laughed for the first time all day. It was a funny name for a bird. 'A booby?'

Timothy was quite serious. 'Dis booby I saw was a blue face, mebbe nestin' out o' Serranilla Bank, mebbe not. Dey by feedin' on d'flyin' feesh. I true watchin' d'birds 'cause dey tell us we veree close to d'shore.'

'How does a booby look, Timothy?'

'Nothin' much,' he replied. 'Tail like our choclade, sharp beak, mos' white on 'is body.'

I tried to picture it, wondering if I'd ever see a bird again.

CHAPTER 6

*I*n the early morning (I knew it was early because the air was still cool and there was dampness on the boards of the raft), I heard Timothy shout, 'I see an islan', true.'

In wild excitement, I stumbled up and fell overboard.

I went under the water, yelling for him, then came up, gasping. I heard a splash and knew he was in the water too.

Something slapped up against my leg, and I thought it was Timothy. I knew how to swim, but didn't know which way to go. So I was treading water. Then I heard Timothy's frightened roar, 'Sharks,' and he was thrashing about near me.

He grabbed my hair with one hand and used his other arm to drag me back towards the raft. I had turned on my face and was trying to hold my breath. Then I felt my body being thrown, and I was back on the boards of the raft, gasping for air. I knew that Timothy was still in the water because I could hear splashing and cursing.

The raft tilted down suddenly on one side. Timothy was back aboard. Panting, he bent over me. He yelled, 'Damn fool mahn! I tol' you 'bout d'shark!'

I knew Timothy was in a rage. I could hear his heavy breathing and knew he was staring at me. 'Shark all 'round us, all d'time,' he roared.

I said, 'I'm sorry.'

Timothy said, 'On dis raff, you crawl, young bahss. You 'ear me?'

I nodded. His voice was thick with anger, but in a moment, after he took several deep breaths, he asked, 'You all right, young bahss?'

I guess he sat down beside me to rest. His breathing was still heavy. Finally, he said, 'Mahn die quick out dere.'

We'd both forgotten about the island. I said, 'Timothy, you saw an island!'

He laughed. 'Yes, d'islan'! Dere 'tis . . .'

I said, 'Where?'

Timothy answered scornfully, 'Dere, look, mahn, look . . .'

Angrily, I said to him, 'I can't see.' He kept forgetting that.

His voice was low when he said, 'Yes, young bahss. Dat be true! In all dis harassment wid d'shark, I did forget.'

Then I felt his hands on my shoulders. He twisted them. 'Dat direction, young bahss.'

Straining to look where he had me pointed, I asked, 'Are there any people on it?'

' 'Tis a veree smahl islan', outrageous low.'

I repeated, 'Are there any people on it.' I thought they could contact my father and then send for help.

Timothy answered honestly, 'No, young bahss. No people. People not be libin' on d'islan' dat 'as no wattah.'

No people. No water. No food. No phones. It was not any better than the raft. In fact, it might be worse. 'How far away are we?'

' 'Bout two mile,' Timothy said.

'Maybe we should stay on the raft. A schooner will see us, or an airplane.'

Timothy said positively, 'No, we bettah off on lan'. An' we driftin' dat way. D'tide be runnin' wid us.' His voice was happy. He wanted to be off the sea.

I was certain my father had planes and ships out looking for us. I said, 'Timothy, the Navy is searching for us. I know.'

Timothy did not answer me. He just said, ' 'Tis a pretty ting, to be sure. I see a white beach, an' behin' dat, low sea-grape bushes; den on d'hill, some palm. Mebbe twenty, thirty palm.'

I was sure he couldn't even see that far.

I said, 'Timothy, wouldn't it be better if we stayed on the raft and found a big island with people on it?'

He ignored me. He said, 'Bidin' d'night, I saw surf washin' white ovah banks off to port, but did not awaken you, young bahss. But knew we be gettin' near d'cays . . .'

I said, 'I don't want to go on that island.'

I don't think there was anyone on earth as stubborn as old Timothy. There was steel in his voice when he answered, 'We be goin' on dat islan' young bahss. Dat be true.'

But he knew how I felt now, because he added, 'From dis islan', we will get help. Be true, I swear . . .'

CHAPTER 7

*I*t seemed hours but it was probably only one until
Timothy said, 'Do not be alarm now, young
bahss. I am goin' to jump into d'wattah an' kick dis
raff to d'shore. Widout dat, we'll pass d'islan', by-'n-
by.'

In a moment, I heard a splash on one side of the raft
and then Timothy's feet began drumming the water. I
guess he was not afraid of sharks this close in. Soon, he
yelled, 'Boddam, young bahss, boddam.' His feet had
touched sand. In another few minutes, the raft lurched
and I knew it had grounded.

I listened for sounds from shore, hoping there would

be a cheerful 'hello', but there were none. Just the wash of the low surf around the raft.

Timothy said, ''Ere, young bahss, on my shoulders an' I'll fetch you to d'lan'.' He helped me to his back.

I said, 'Don't forget Stew Cat.'

He laughed back heartily. 'One at a time, young bahss.'

With me on his back, he splashed ashore, and judging from the time it took, the raft wasn't very far out. Then he lifted me down again.

'Lan',' he shouted,

The warm sand did feel good on my feet and now I was almost glad that we wouldn't have to spend another night on the hard, wet boards of the raft.

He said, 'Touch it, young bahss. Feel d'lan', 'tis outrageous good.'

I reached down. The grains of sand felt very fine, almost like powder.

Timothy said, ''Tis a beautiful cay, dis cay. Nevah hab I seen dis cay.' Then he led me to sit under a clump of bushes. He said, 'You res' easy while I pull d'raff more out of d'wattah. We mus' not lose it.'

I sat there in the shade, running sand through my fingers, wondering where, among all those many islands in the Caribbean, we were.

Timothy shouted up from the water, 'Many feesh 'ere. *Langosta*, too, I b'knowin'. We ros' dem.'

Langosta, I knew, was the native lobster, the one without claws. I heard Timothy splashing around down by the surf and knew he was pulling the raft up as far as he could get it.

A moment later, puffing hard, he flopped down beside me. He said, 'Cotch me breath, den I will tour d'islan', an' select a place for camp . . .'

He put Stew Cat into my lap.

'Camp?' I asked, stroking big Stew.

Timothy replied, 'We mebbe 'ere two, tree days. So we be libin' comfortable.'

He could tell I was discouraged because we had come to the island and there were no people on it. He said confidently, 'We be rescue, true. Before d'night, I build a great fire pile o' brush an' wood. So d'nex' aircraft dat fly ovah, we set it off.'

'Where are we, Timothy? Near Panama?'

He answered slowly, 'I cannot be sure, young bahss. Not veree sure.'

'But you said you knew about the banks and the cays that are near the banks.' I wondered if he knew anything, really, or if he was just a stupid old black man.

Timothy said, 'Lissen, I know dat many banks an' cays are roun' fifteen north an' eighty long. Dere is Roncador an' Serrann; Quito Sueño an' Serranilla an' Rosalind; den dere is Beacon an' North Cay. Off to d'wes', somewhere, is Providencia an' San Andrés . . .' He paused a moment and then said, 'Far 'way, up dere, I tink, is d'Caymens, an' den Jamaica.'

'But you are not sure of this island?'

Timothy answered gravely, 'True, I am not sure.'

'Do the schooners usually come close by here?' I asked.

Again very gravely, Timothy said, 'D'mahn who feeshes follows d'feesh. Sartainly, d'feesh be 'ere. I be seein' wid my own self eyes.'

I kept feeling that Timothy was holding something back from me. It was the tone of his voice. I'd heard my father talk that way a few times. Once, when he didn't want to tell me my grandfather was about to die; another time was when a car ran over my dog in Virginia.

Of course, both times happened when I was younger. Now, my father was always honest with me, I thought, because he said that in the end that was better. I wished Timothy would be honest with me.

Instead he got up to take a walk around the cay, saying he'd be back in a few minutes. Then Stew Cat wandered away. I called to him but he seemed to be exploring too. Realizing that I was alone on the beach I became frightened.

I knew how helpless I was without Timothy. First I began calling for Stew Cat but when he didn't return I began shouting for Timothy. There was no answer. I wondered if he'd fallen down and was hurt. I began to crawl along the beach and ran head on into a clump of low hanging brush.

I sat down again, batting at gnats that were buzzing around my face. Something brushed against my arm, and I yelled out in terror. But I heard a meow and knew it was only Stew Cat. I reached for him and held him tight until I heard the brush crackling and sang out, 'Timothy?'

'Yes, young bahss,' he called back from quite a distance.

When he was closer, I said harshly, 'Never leave me again. Don't you ever leave me again!'

He laughed. 'Dere is nothin' to fear 'ere. I walked roun' d'whole islan', an' dere is nothin' but sea grape, sand, a few lil' lizzard, an' dose palm tree . . .'

I repeated, 'Never leave me alone, Timothy.'

'All right, young bahss, I promise,' he said.

He must have been looking all around, for he said, 'No wattah 'ere, but 'tis no problem. We still 'ave wattah in d'kag, an' we will trap more on d'firs' rain.'

Still believing he wasn't telling me everything, I said, 'You were gone a long time.'

He answered uneasily, 'Thirty minutes at mos'. D'islan' is 'bout one mile long, an' a half wide, shaped like d'melon. I foun' a place to make our camp, up near d'palm. 'Twill be a good place for a lookout. D'rise is 'bout forty feet from d'sea.'

I nodded, then said, 'I'm hungry, Timothy.'

We were both hungry. He went back to the raft, took out the keg of water and the tin of biscuits and chocolate.

While we were eating, I said, 'You are worried about something, Timothy. Please tell me the truth. I'm old enough to know.'

Timothy waited a long time before answering, probably trying to choose the right words. Finally, he said, 'Young bahss, dere is, in dis part of d'sea, a few lil' cays like dis one, surround on bot' sides by hombug banks. Dey are cut off from d'res' o' d'sea by dese banks . . .'

I tried to make a mental picture of that. Several small islands tucked up inside great banks of coral that made navigation dangerous was what I finally decided on.

'You think we are on one of those cays?'

'Mebbe, young bahss, mebbe.'

Fear coming back to me – I knew he'd made a mistake in bringing us ashore – I said, 'Then no ships will pass even close to us. Not even schooners! We're trapped here!' We might live here for ever, I thought.

Again he did not answer directly. I was beginning to learn that he had a way of being honest while still being dishonest. He said, 'D'place I am tinking of is call Debil's Mout', 'Tis a U-shaped ting, wit dese sharp coral banks on either side, runnin' maybe forty, fifty mile . . .'

He let that sink in. It sounded bad. But then he said, 'I do hope, young bahss, dat I am outrageous mistaken.'

'If we are in the Devil's Mouth, how can we be rescued?' I asked angrily. It was his fault we were there.

'D'fire pile! When aircraft fly above, dey will see d'smoke an' fire!'

'But they might just think it is a native fisherman. No one else could come here!'

I could picture him nodding, thinking about that. Finally, he said, 'True, but we cannot fret 'bout it, can we? We'll make camp, an' see what 'appens.'

He poured me a half cup of water, saying happily, 'Since we 'ave made lan', we can celebrate.'

I drank it slowly and thoughtfully.

CHAPTER 8

*D*uring the afternoon, Timothy was busy and we did not talk much. He was making a hut of dried palm fronds. I sat near him under a palm. Now that we were on shore, I again began to think about what had happened to my mother. Somehow, I felt she was safe. I was also sure that a search had been started for us, not fully understanding that a war was on and that all the ships and aircraft were needed to fight the U-boats. I even thought about Henrik van Boven and what a story I would have to tell when I saw him again.

I tried not to think about my eyes, sitting there under the palm, listening to Timothy hum as he made the camp. I trusted him that my sight would return within a few days. I also trusted him that an aircraft would spot our fire pile.

In late afternoon, he said proudly, 'Look, our hut!'

I had to remind him again, stupid old man, that I couldn't see, so he took my hands and ran them over the fronds. It was a hut, he said, about eight feet wide and six feet deep, with supports made of wood he'd picked off the beach. The supports were tied together with strong vines that covered the north end of the island.

The roof, which sloped back, he said, was about six feet off the ground. I could easily stand up in it, but Timothy couldn't. Not quite.

Timothy said, 'Tomorrow, we be gettin' mats to sleep on, weave our own, but tonight we mus' sleep on d'sand. 'Tis soft.'

I knew he was very proud of the hut. It had taken him only a few hours to build it.

'Now,' he said, 'I mus' go downg to d'reef an' fetch langosta. We'll ros' it, to be true.'

I became frightened again the minute he said it. I didn't want to be left alone, and I was afraid something might happen to him. 'Take me with you, Timothy,' I pleaded.

'Not on d'reef,' he answered firmly. 'I 'ave not been dere before. If 'tis safe, tomorrow I will take you.' With that, he went down the hill without saying another word.

My mother was right, I thought. They had their

place and we had ours. He did not really like me, or he would have taken me along. He was different.

It seemed as though he were gone for a very long time. Once, I thought I heard an aircraft, but it was probably just my imagination. I began yelling for Timothy to come back, but I guess he couldn't hear because of water noise on the reef.

The palm fronds above me rattled in the breeze, and there were other noises from the underbrush. I knew Stew Cat was around somewhere, but it didn't sound like him.

I wondered if Timothy had checked for snakes. There were also scorpions on most Caribbean islands, and they were deadly. I wondered if there were any on our cay.

During those first few days on the island, the times I spent alone were terrible. It was, of course, being unable to see that made all the sounds so frightening. I guess if you are born blind, it is not so bad. You grow up knowing each sound and what it means.

Suddenly, the tears came out. I knew it was not a manly thing to do, something my father would have frowned on, but I couldn't stop. Then from nowhere came Stew Cat. He rubbed along my arms and up against my cheek, purring hard. I held him close.

Soon, Timothy came up the hill, shouting, 'Young bahss, tree nice langosta.'

I refused to speak to him because he had left me for such a long time.

He stood over me and said, ''Ere, touch dem, dey are still alive.' He was almost crowing over his lobster.

I turned away. Sooner or later, Timothy would have

to understand that he could not ignore me one minute and then, treat me as a friend the next.

He said softly, 'Young bahss, be an outrageous mahn if you like, but 'ere I'm all you got.'

I didn't answer.

He roasted the langosta over the fire, and later we crawled into the hut to spend our first night on the silent island.

Timothy seemed very tired and groaned a lot. Before we went to sleep, I asked him, 'Tell me the truth, Timothy, how old are you?'

He sighed deeply, 'More dan seventy. Eben more dan seventy . . .'

He was very old. Old enough to die there.

In the morning, Timothy began making the fire pile down on the beach. He had a plan. We'd always keep a small fire smouldering up by the hut, and if an airplane came near, he'd take a piece of burning wood from our small fire to ignite the big one. That way, he said, we could save the few matches that we had.

It didn't take him long to stack driftwood over dried palm fronds. Then he said, 'Now, young bahss, we mus' say somethin' on d'san'.'

Sometimes it was difficult to understand Timothy. The soft and beautiful West Indian accent and way of speaking weren't always clear.

'Say something on the sand?' I asked.

'So dey be knowin' we are downg 'ere,' he explained patiently.

'Who?'

'D'mahn in d'sky, of course.'

'Oh.' Now I understood.

I guess Timothy was standing there looking at me, waiting for me to say something or do something. I heard him say, 'Well, young bahss.'

'What do we do now?' I asked.

His voice now impatient, he said, 'Say somethin' wid d'rock, wid many rock; eeevery rock be sayin' somethin' . . .'

I frowned at him. 'I don't think I can help you, Timothy. I can't see any rocks.'

Timothy groaned. 'I can see d'rock, young bahss. But what do we say?'

I laughed at him, enjoying it now. 'We say "help".'

He grunted satisfaction.

For the next twenty or thirty minutes, I could hear Timothy dropping rocks against each other, singing softly to himself in calypso. It was a song about 'fungee an' feesh.' I'd had 'fungi' in Willemstad down in the blacks' market at Ruyterkade. It was just plain old corn meal. But most food has different names in the islands.

Soon, he came to stand over me. 'Now, young bahss,' he said. He seemed to be waiting.

'Yes?'

There was a silence until Timothy broke it with anguish, 'Wid d'rock, say "help".'

I looked up in his direction and suddenly understood that Timothy could not spell. He was just too stubborn, or too proud, to admit it.

I nodded and began feeling around the sand for a stick.

He asked, 'What you reachin' for?'

'A stick to make lines with.'

He placed one in my hands, and I carefully lettered H-E-L-P on the sand while he stood above me, watching. He kept murmuring, 'Ah-huh, ah-huh,' as if making sure I was spelling it correctly.

When I had finished, Timothy said approvingly, 'I tell you, young bahss, dat do say help.' Then he happily arranged the rocks on the sand, following my lines.

I felt good. I knew how to do something that Timothy couldn't do. *He couldn't spell*. I felt superior to Timothy that day, but I let him play his little game, pretending not to know that he really couldn't spell.

CHAPTER 9

*I*n the afternoon, Timothy said we'd make a rope.
On the north end of the island, tough vines, almost as large as a pencil, were laced over the sand. It took us several hours to tear out a big pile of them. Then Timothy began weaving a rope that would stretch all the way down the hill to the beach and fire pile.

The rope was for me. If he happened to be out on the reef, and I heard a plane, I could take a light from our campfire, follow the rope down, and touch off the big fire. The vine rope would also serve to get me safely down to the beach.

After we'd torn the vines out, and he was weaving

the rope, he said, 'Young bahss, you mus' begin to help wid d'udder wark.'

We were sitting up by the hut. I had my back to a palm and was thinking that back in Willemstad, at this moment, I'd probably be sitting in a classroom, three desks away from Henrik, listening to Herr Jonckheer talk about European history. I'd been tutored in Dutch the first year in Willemstad so I could attend the regular school. Now I could speak it and understand it.

My hands were tired from pulling the vines, and I just wanted to sit and think. I didn't want to work. I said, 'Timothy, I'm blind. I can't see to work.'

I heard him cutting something with his sharp knife. He replied softly, 'D'han' is not blin'.'

Didn't the old man understand? To work, aside from pulling up vines or drawing something in the sand, you must be able to see.

Stubbornly, he said, 'Young bahss, we need sleepin' mats. You can make d'mats.'

I looked over in his direction. 'You do it,' I said.

He sighed back, saying, 'D'best matmaker in Charlotte Amalie, downg in Frenchtown, b'total blin'.'

'But he's a man, and he has to do that to make a living.'

'B'true,' Timothy said quietly.

But in a few minutes, he placed several lengths of palm fibre across my lap. He really was a black mule. 'D'palm mat is veree easy. Jus' ovah an' under . . .'

Becoming angry with him, I said, 'I tell you, I can't see.'

He paid no attention to me. 'Take dis han' hol'
d'palm like dis; den ovah an' under, like d'mahn in
Frenchtown; den more palm.'

I could feel him standing there watching me as I
tried to reeve the lengths, but I knew they weren't
fitting together. He said, 'Like dis, I tell you,' and
reached down to guide my hand. 'Ovah an' under . . .'

I tried again, but it didn't work. I stood up, threw
the palm fibres at him, and screamed, 'You ugly black
man! I won't do it! You're stupid, you can't even
spell . . .'

Timothy's heavy hand struck my face sharply.

Stunned, I touched my face where he'd hit me. Then
I turned away from where I thought he was. My cheek
stung, but I wouldn't let him see me with tears in my
eyes.

I heard him saying very gently, 'B'gettin' back to
wark, my own self.'

I sat down again.

He began to sing that 'fungee and feesh' song in a
low voice, and I could picture him sitting on the sand
in front of the hut; that tangled grey hair, the ugly
black face with the thick lips, those great horny hands
winding the strands of vine.

The rope, I thought. It wasn't for him. It was for me.

After a while, I said, 'Timothy . . .'

He did not answer, but walked over to me, pressing
more palm fronds into my hands. He murmured, ''Tis
veree easy, ovah an' under . . .' Then he went back to
singing about fungee and feesh.

Something happened to me that day on the cay. I'm not quite sure what it was even now, but I had begun to change.

I said to Timothy, 'I want to be your friend.'

He said softly, 'Young bahss, you 'ave always been my friend.'

I said, 'Can you call me Phillip instead of young boss?'

'Phill-eep,' he said warmly.

CHAPTER 10

During our seventh night on the island, it rained. It was one of those tropical storms that come up swiftly without warning. We were asleep on the palm mats that I'd made, but it awakened us immediately. The rain sounded like bullets hitting on the dried palm frond roof. We ran out into it, shouting and letting the fresh water hit our bodies. It was cool and felt good.

Timothy yelled that his catchment was working. He had taken more boards from the top of the raft and had made a large trough that would catch the rain. He'd picked up bamboo lengths on the beach and had fitted them together into a short pipe to funnel the rain water into our ten-gallon keg.

It rained for almost two hours, and Timothy was quite angry with himself for not making a second catchment because the keg was soon filled and overflowing.

We stayed out in the cool rain for twenty or thirty minutes and then went back inside. The roof leaked badly but we didn't mind. We got on our mats and opened our mouths to the sweet, fresh water. Stew Cat was huddled in a miserable ball over in a corner, Timothy said, not enjoying it at all.

I liked the rain because it was something I could hear and feel; not something I must see. It peppered in bursts against the frond roof, and I could hear the drips as it leaked through. The squall wind was in the tops of the palms and I could imagine how they looked in the night sky, thrashing against each other high over our little cay.

I wanted it to rain all night.

We talked for a long time when the rain began to slack off. Timothy asked me about my mother and father. I told him all about them and about how we lived in Scharloo, getting very lonesome and homesick while I was telling him. He kept saying, 'Ah, dat be true?'

Then Timothy told me what he could remember from his own childhood. It wasn't at all like mine. He'd never gone to school, and was working on a fishing boat by the time he was ten. It almost seemed the only fun he had was once a year at carnival when he'd put frangipani leaves around his ankles and dress up in a donkey hide to parade around with *mocki jumbis*, the spirit chasers, while the old ladies of Charlotte Amalie danced the *bambola* around them.

He chuckled. 'I drink plenty rhum dose tree days of carnival.'

I could picture him in his donkey skin, wheeling around to the music of the steel bands. They had them in Willemstad too.

Because it had been on my mind I told him that my mother didn't like black people and asked him why.

He answered slowly, 'I don' like some white people my own self, but 'twould be outrageous if I didn' like any o' dem.'

Wanting to hear it from Timothy, I asked him why there were different colours of skin, white and black, brown and red, and he laughed back, 'Why b'feesh different colour, or flower b'different colour? I true don' know, Phill-eep, but I true tink beneath d'skin is all d'same.'

Herr Jonckheer had said something like that in school but it did not mean quite as much as when Timothy said it.

Long after he'd begun to snore in the dripping hut, I thought about it. Suddenly, I wished my father and mother could see us there together on the little island.

I moved close to Timothy's big body before I went to sleep. I remember smiling in the darkness. He felt neither white nor black.

★

In the morning, the air was crisp and the cay smelled fresh and clean. Timothy cooked a small fish, a pompano, that he'd speared at dawn down on the reef. Neither of us had felt so good or so clean since we had been aboard the *Hato*. And without discussing it, we both thought this might be the day an aircraft would swing up into the Devil's Mouth, if that's where we were.

The pompano, broiled over the low fire, tasted good. Of course, we were eating little but what came from the sea. Fish, langosta, mussels, or the eggs from sea urchins, those small, black round sea animals with sharp spines that attach themselves to the reefs.

Timothy had tried to make a stew from seaweed but it tasted bitter. Then he'd tried to boil some new sea-grape roots but they made us ill. The only thing that ever worked for him was sea-grape leaves, boiled first in sea water and then cooked in fresh water.

But above us, forty feet from the ground, Timothy said, was a feast. Big, fat green coconuts. When we'd landed there were a few dried ones on the ground, but the meat in them was not very tasty. In a fresher one, there was still some milk, but it was rancid.

At least once a day, especially when we were around the hut, Timothy would say. ''Tis outrageous dem coconut hang up in d'sky when we could use d'milk an' meat.' Or he'd say, 'Timothy, my own self, long ago could climb d'palm veree easy.' Or hinting, and I guess looking up at them, 'Phill-eep, I do believe you b'gettin' outrageous strong 'ere on d'islan'.'

He made a point of saying that if he were only fifty again he could climb the tree and slice them off with his knife. But at seventy-odd, he did not think he could make it to the top.

That morning over breakfast, Timothy said, looking to the tops of the palms, I'm sure, 'A lil' milk from d'coconut would b'good now, eh, Phill-eep?'

As yet, I didn't have the courage to climb the palms. 'Yes, it would,' I said.

Timothy cleared his throat, sighed deeply, and put the coconuts out of his mind. But I knew he'd try me again.

He said, 'Dem devilin' coconuts aside, your mutthur would never be knowin' you now.'

I asked why.

'You are veree brown an' veree lean,' he said.

I tried to imagine how I looked. I knew my shirt and pants were in tatters. My hair felt ropy. There was no way to comb it. I wondered how my eyes looked and asked Timothy about that.

'Dey look widout cease,' he said. 'Dey stare, Phill-eep.'

'Do they bother you?'

Timothy laughed. 'Not me. Eeevery day I tink what rare good luck I 'ave dat you be 'ere wid my own self on dis outrageous, hombug islan'.'

I thought awhile and then asked him, 'How long was it before that friend of yours, that friend in the Barbados, could see again?'

Timothy replied vaguely, 'Oh, many mont', I do recall.'

'But you told me on the raft it was only three days.'

'Did I say dat?'

'Yes!'

'Well,' Timothy said, ''twas a long time ago. But 'e got 'is sight back, to be true.' He paused a moment, then said, 'Now, I tell you, we got much wark to do today.'

I noticed more and more that Timothy always changed the subject when we began to talk about my eyes. He would make any kind of an excuse.

'What work?' I asked.

'Now, lemme see,' he said. 'For one ting, we mus' make another catchment . . . an' we mus' go to d'reef for food . . . an' . . .'

I waited.

Timothy finally exploded. 'Now, dat is a lot o' wark, Phill-eep, to be true.'

CHAPTER 11

T imothy had fashioned a cane for me, and I was now using it to feel my way around the island. I fell down often, but unless I fell into sea grape, it did not hurt. Even then, I only got a few scratches.

Slowly, I was beginning to know the island. By myself, keeping my feet in the damp sand, which meant I was near the water, I walked the whole way around it. Timothy was very proud of me.

From walking over it, feeling it, and listening to it, I think I knew what our cay looked like. As Timothy said, it was shaped like a melon, or a turtle, sloped up from the sea to our ridge where the palms

67

flapped all day and night in the light trade wind.

The beach, I now believed, was about forty yards wide in most places, stretching all the way around the island. On one end, to the east, was a low coral reef that extended several hundred yards, awash in many places.

I know it was to the east because one morning I was down there with Timothy when the sun came up, and I could feel the warmth on my face from that direction.

The sea grape, a few feet tall at the edge of the beach, and higher farther back, grew along the slopes of the hill on all sides. There was also some other brush that did not feel like sea grape, but Timothy did not know the name of it.

To the south, the beach sloped gradually out into the water. On the north side, it was different. There were submerged coral reefs and great shelves. The water became deep very abruptly. Timothy warned against going into the water here because the sharks could swim close to the shore.

Timothy said that the water all around the cay was clear and that he could see many beautiful fish. There was brain coral and organ-pipe coral that the parrot fish would nibble.

From what I could feel and hear, our cay seemed a lovely island and I wished that I could see it. I planned to walk around it at least once a day, following the vine rope from the ridge to the beach, then setting out along the sand.

I was starting to be less dependent on the vine rope,

and sometimes it seemed to me that Timothy was trying hard to make me independent of him. I thought I knew why, but I did not talk to him about it. I did not want to think about the possibility of Timothy dying and leaving me alone on the cay.

Because the rain the night before had made us hopeful, I think both of us did our chores with one ear to the sky, listening for the sound of engines. But all day we heard nothing but familiar sounds, the surf, the wind, and the cries of sea birds.

That night after dinner, Timothy grumbled, 'No aircraft! D'islan' mus' 'ave a jumbi.'

'Don't talk nonsense, Timothy,' I said.

'D'evil spirit harass an' meliss us,' he said darkly. 'An' we do not 'ave a chicken or grains o' corn to chase 'im.'

I said, 'Timothy, you can't really believe in that.'

My father had told me about 'obediah', or 'voodoo', in the West Indies. It had come over from Africa, of course. Haiti was the worst of all for it, but there was some practice on all the islands. It was mixed up with religion and witch doctors.

I knew he was looking at Stew Cat when he said, 'Mebbe dat outrageous cat is d'jumbi.'

'He's just an old cat, Timothy,' I protested.

Recalling everything that had happened, Timothy said, 'He came board d'raff, an' we got separated from all else; den d'young bahss' eyes got dark, gibbin' us exceedin' trouble; den we float up dis hombuggin' Debil's Mout'. . . .'

Angrily, I said, 'Timothy, Stew Cat is not a jumbi. You let him alone.'

The old man was silent, and I was suddenly worried for Stew Cat's safety. Timothy stayed by me all night but in the morning, when I awakened, he was gone and so was Stew Cat.

I crawled out of the hut and began to call for Stew. Then I called for Timothy. There was no answer. I went down the hill and headed up the beach towards the reef. Voodoo was silly, I knew, but it was also frightening. I couldn't understand why Timothy thought Stew Cat was the jumbi.

I decided to circle the island to find them. Using my cane to feel the way, to touch driftwood or coral ledges the night tide might have uncovered, I moved along the damp sand, calling out now and then.

When I reached the north side, Timothy answered, 'Marnin', Phill-eep.'

I asked him where he'd been.

He laughed. 'Dere is lil' place to go 'ere. I 'ave been 'ere on dis beach.'

'Where is Stew Cat?'

Timothy was silent.

I asked again.

'B'gettin' his own self a lizzard, mebbe, mebbe,' he answered, but there was something conniving in his voice.

All the while, I could hear a scraping noise and, occasionally, a ring of metal. 'What are you doing?' I asked.

'Cuttin' on an ol' piece o' wood,' he replied.

Why would he be down on north beach this early cutting wood? I knew we had plenty for the campfire and the signal fire.

'And you haven't seen Stew Cat?'

'Not a 'air,' he said.

I wanted to see what he had in his hands, but I didn't have the courage to walk up and touch it. I said, 'Timothy, I'm very hungry.'

I felt his hand on my wrist. He said, 'We'll go to d'hut.'

He fixed breakfast, we ate, and then without a word, he slipped away.

Usually, he kept his hunting knife in the tin box that had stored our biscuits. Also in that box were the dry matches we had left, a few pieces of stale chocolate, and small things that Timothy had salvaged from the beach or the raft.

I felt a few nails, the hinges that had been on the raft's trap door, some short lengths of rope, a piece of cork, several small tin cans, and a small roll of something that felt like leather. Nothing was missing except the knife, and I knew he'd taken it to north beach with him.

As best I could, I searched around the hut area for Stew Cat, thinking maybe Timothy had tied him up somewhere. Yet I was certain he'd be meowing if he was within hearing distance.

I was positive that Timothy was back on north beach cutting on that piece of wood but something told me not to go down there. So I sat by the hut wondering what to do. It was no good trying to convince him that jumbi did not exist, nor was there any way to find Stew Cat if Timothy had hidden him.

The morning hours passed slowly. Once, I went down to east beach to sit near the signal fire, hoping to hear the drone of an aircraft. Several times, over the stir of the wind, I thought I heard a faint meow, but I couldn't locate the direction.

Maybe all that had happened was beginning to work on the old man's mind. Maybe I was stranded on a tiny, forgotten island in the Caribbean with a madman. If he harmed Stew Cat because of some silly jumbi thing, I knew he might also harm me.

I thought about getting back on the raft and letting it drift to sea again. I was certain that there were enough boards still on top to sit and sleep on. If I could get the water keg down the hill, and the last pieces of chocolate out of the box, I'd be all right for a few days.

I got up and went down to the water, feeling my way towards the reef. I knew that if I kept going that way, I'd touch or fall over the length of life-line rope that tethered the raft. Timothy had driven a heavy piece of driftwood into the sand so that the raft would not go out to sea with the tide.

I walked slowly and carefully, expecting at any moment to feel the rope with my cane, or have it hit against my ankles. I went all the way to the beginning of the reef without finding it. Then I reversed my course, and walked in the other direction. Finally, I stumbled over the heavy piece of wood that Timothy had driven into the sand.

I felt around it, but the rope was no longer tied to it. He'd cut the raft loose! Panic swept over me. But taking my bearing from the stake, I decided to go out into the water, hoping to find the raft.

A few feet offshore, I got another bad scare. I put my foot down and something moved. In fact the whole bottom seemed to move. I lost my balance and fell headfirst into the water. I came up sputtering, and realized I'd stepped on a skate, that diamond-shaped fish with a stinger tail. I'd done that once or twice at Westpunt. The skate is kin to the deadly sea ray, but this one was as shocked as I was and swam off to deep water.

I went out to my waist, feeling with my hands in all directions. But the raft was gone!

I trusted Timothy, and kept telling myself that he wouldn't harm me, but it was the whole mysterious jumbi thing that was frightening. And he certainly wasn't acting like the Timothy I'd been living with.

In mid-afternoon he returned to the hut. Neither of us spoke.

Then I heard him pounding something. The palm fronds on the hut rattled; whatever it was, he was pounding it into the hut. Having finished, he went away again.

When I heard him moving through the sea grape down the path, I got up and began feeling around the framing of the hut. There was nothing on the sides of it, and I decided that whatever he'd attached had to be on the roof.

I knew there were several lengths of log over near the campfire. So I approached it, found one of the logs, and rolled it over to the entrance to the hut. I stood on it and felt along the cross-frame that held the roof up.

In the very centre I found what I was looking for. I cried out when the palm of my hand touched something sharp. Then with my fingers, I slowly felt around the object. It had a head, I discovered, four feet, and a tail.

Timothy had spent all that time carving a cat, a Stew Cat. The nails in it were supposed to kill the evil jumbi.

I felt weak and sat down on the log.

Soon, he came up the path, dropping Stew Cat into my lap.

'Where was he?' I asked.

'On d'raff, o'course,' Timothy answered. 'I got 'im off d'islan' till I could chase d'jumbi.'

'Where is the raft, Timothy?'

''Twas off d'shore, Phill-eep. 'Tis back now. An' our luck is change.'

But it didn't change. It got worse.

CHAPTER 12

One morning in the middle of May, I awakened to hear Timothy taking great breaths. It sounded as though he were fighting for air. I listened a moment and then asked, 'Are you all right, Timothy?'

He wheezed back, 'Feber! Malar!'

I had to think a moment to understand what he was talking about. Fever! Malaria! I reached over to touch him. His forehead was burning hot.

His breath coming in big, harsh sighs, he said, 'I got malar agin, Phill-eep. 'Twill go away, but fetch some wattah.'

When I had had fever in Virginia, and at Scharloo,

my mother had given me aspirin and then put cold cloths on my head. But we had no aspirin on the cay, of course, and the water was always warm. I poured some water from the keg, and gave it to him. He gulped it and then fell back on the mat.

For a while, I listened to his heavy breathing and then ripped a piece of cloth from what was left of my shirt, dampened it with water, and placed it on his forehead. He murmured, 'Dat be good,' but suddenly he began to shiver, even though the morning air was already warm. I could hear his teeth clacking.

I had nothing to cover him with, so I just sat beside him holding the cloth, which was already beginning to dry, to his forehead. His breath was like air from a furnace.

It must have been about ten o'clock when Timothy began to mumble and laugh. It sounded almost as if he were talking in his sleep, but the laughter, little bursts of it between the wheezes, was very high and strange. I couldn't keep the cloth on his head because he was tossing from side to side.

I talked to him constantly, but he didn't even seem to know I was there.

Once he got up but fell back down to the mat, and I told him to stay very still. For a long time, he did, because he began to shiver again. When that ended, the mumbling and high laughter started all over.

At about noontime, the mumbling got worse, and I could feel him trying to get to his feet. I clung to his arm, shouting for him to lie down again, but he threw me aside as if I weren't there. I could hear him crashing down the hill towards the sea, the frightening laughter echoing back.

I followed the trail of laughter. Then I heard splashing and knew he'd gone into the water. I yelled, 'Timothy, Timothy, come back.'

Suddenly it became dead quiet. I screamed his name again and again. There was no answer.

I reached the beach and waded out to my knees, then began to move slowly along, trying to keep on a line with the beach. I had gone about thirty steps when I fell over Timothy's body, plunging down in the water.

Holding on to him with one hand, I got on my feet again. The upper part of his body was floating but I knew his feet were dragging on the bottom. I put my face against his mouth. Yes, he was still breathing.

I worked myself around to put both hands under his shoulders, but he was too heavy that way. Then I clasped my hands under his chin, and began to pull him out. He made strange sounds, but did not try to help me.

It took me what seemed like a long time to get Timothy out of the water and back up on the damp sand. He must have weighed two hundred and twenty or thirty pounds, and I could only move him two or three inches at a time.

I sat beside him for almost an hour in the hot sun while he rested quietly, his breathing not so harsh now. Then I realized he was shivering again. I knew I could not drag him up the slope to the shelter of the hut, so I tore off branches of sea grape and put them over his body. The grape leaves cut the rays of the sun.

I brought water down from the hut, raised his head, and ordered him to drink it. With one hand, I found his lips and then guided the cup to his chin. He seemed to understand and gulped it down.

I stayed by him the rest of the long afternoon while he slept. When he awakened, it was early evening and had turned cool again. He was breathing easily now, and I knew the fever had broken because his forehead was no longer hot.

Sitting up, he said weakly, 'How did I get downg 'ere?'

I told him he'd run down the hill.

'Dat debil, d'fever,' Timothy sighed.

I said, 'You went into the water. You scared me, Timothy.'

'Dat be true,' he said. 'My 'ead burn wid fire, an' I put it out.'

I helped him to his feet, and we went up the hill together, Timothy leaning on me for support for the first time. He never really regained his strength.

CHAPTER 13

*I*t was in late May that I believe Timothy decided
we might stay there for ever. We had not seen a
schooner sail or heard an airplane since setting foot on
the island.

l know it was late May because each day he dropped
a small pebble into an old can that he'd found on the
beach. It was our only way to tell how many days
we'd been there. Every so often, I'd count them,
beginning with 9 April. We now had forty-eight pebbles in the can.

On this day, Timothy said thoughtfully, 'Phill-eep,
'as it evah come into your own self that I might be

poorly again some marnin'?' I knew he was thinking about malar and the fever.

I said it had.

He said, 'Well, you mus' den know how to provite your own self wid feesh.'

For more than a week, I knew he had been labouring over nails to turn them into fish hooks. He always speared the fish or langosta with a sharp stick, but I could not see, of course, to do that. I knew he was making the hooks for me.

He said, with a secret tone in his voice, 'I 'ave foun' an outrageous good 'ole on d'reef in a safe place.'

We went down the hill and started out along the reef shelf. By now, my feet were tough and I hardly felt the jagged edges of the coral. But I knew that lurking in the tide pools were the treacherous sea urchins. Stepping on them invited a sharp spine in your foot, and Timothy had already warned me that, 'dey veree poison, dey b'gibbin' you terrible pain.'

Every two feet, Timothy had driven a piece of driftwood deep into the coral crevices so that I could feel them as I went along. Neither of us knew what to do about the sea urchins but Timothy said he'd think mightily about them. He had taken a large rock to smash them all along the path over the reef top. But in time they would come back.

We went out about fifty feet along the reef, and then he said, 'Now, we feesh.'

He described the hole to me. It was about twenty feet in diameter and six to eight feet deep. The bottom was sandy, but mostly free of coral so that my hooks would not snag. He said there was a 'mos' natural opening to the sea, so that the fish could swim in and out of this coral-walled pool.

He took my hand to have me feel all around the edges of the hole. The coral had been smoothed over by centuries of sea wash. Timothy said that the sand in the sea water acted like a grindstone on the sharp edges of the coral. It was not completely smooth but there were no jagged edges sticking out.

'Now, reach downg 'ere,' Timothy said, 'an' tug off d' mussel.'

I put my hand into the warm water, kneeling down over the ledge, and felt a mussel. But in ripping it loose, I lost my balance and only Timothy's hand prevented me from falling in. If you are blind, the sensation of falling can be terrifying. My memory of the fall off the raft was still very clear.

Timothy said, 'Easy dere, Phill-eep. Jus' sit a moment an' relax.'

His voice was soothing. 'If evah you do fall, jus' stay in d'hole awhile, feel which way d'wattah washes, den follow it to d'ledge, grab hol', an' pull your own self out.'

Timothy guided my hands in opening the tough mussel shell and digging the slippery meat out to bait the hook. ''Tis an outrageous sharp knife, so be veree careful o' your fingers.'

Then he told me to feel the hook and slip the mussel bait over the barb. I'd fished many times with my father and this was easy.

Rusty bolts served as sinkers. Timothy had found several pieces of wood with bolts in them; had burned them, then raked the bolts out of the ashes. He'd unravelled a lifeline from the raft to make single strands for the fishing line.

I dropped the hook and sinker overboard. In a moment, there was a sharp tug. I jerked, flipping the fish back over my shoulder so it would land on the reef. Timothy cheered and told me to feel along the line to the wriggling fish, then take the hook out.

Squirming and jumping in my hand, it was small but fat. I grinned over towards Timothy. When I had fished before, it was fun. Now, I felt I had done something very special. I was learning to do things all over again, by touch and feel.

I said to Timothy, 'Dis is outrageous, hombuggin' good feesh 'ole.'

He laughed with pleasure.

Every day after that I did all the fishing. Timothy, of course, continued to get langosta. He had to dive for them, but I caught all the fish. After the third morning, he let me go out alone on the reef. I'd feel my way along his driftwood stobs, find the hole, pry a mussel loose, and then fish.

I was alone on the reef but somehow I always felt he was sitting on the beach nearby. I could sense his presence, yet he was always at the hut when I got back there.

We often talked about the cay and what was on it. Timothy had not thought much about it. He took it for granted that the cay was always there, but I told him about geography, and how maybe a volcano could have caused the Devil's Mouth. He'd listen in fascination, almost speechless.

We talked about how the little coral animals might have been building the foundations of the cay for thousands of years. I said, 'Then sand began to gather on it, and after more years, it was finally an island.'

It was as if a new world had opened up for Timothy. He kept using that same expression, 'Dat be true?'

I found out that he'd never thought about how the sea grape, or the vines, or the coconuts came to our cay. I told him what I knew.

Seeds had drifted in from the sea, or birds had brought them. After a rain, they'd taken root.

'D'lizzard?' he asked sternly.

'I'd bet a bird, flying from another island, holding a mother lizard in its beak, dropped it here. Then the baby lizards were born. Or maybe a mother lizard washed ashore on driftwood during a storm.'

Timothy was very impressed, and I felt good that I'd been able to tell him something.

We found a lot to talk about.

I think it was the fifth afternoon of this week that I blurted out to Timothy, 'I'll climb the palm now.'

'Eh, Phill-eep,' he said, and I could almost see the grin on his face and the light in his eyes as he looked skywards. Greedily, I'm sure.

He said, 'Dere is one coconut tree ovah dere dat 'as a sway in 'is back like an ol' horse. Dat is d'one to clim'.'

I was trembling a little as he led me to the tree, telling me I should go up just a short way; climb it like a monkey. If I could do it, I was to come back down, put the knife between my teeth, and go up again.

The trunk of this palm tree must have been about two feet in diameter because I could easily put my hands around to the back. I grasped it, hunched my body, placed my bare feet on the rough trunk, and began to climb. Timothy was probably holding his breath.

I went up about ten feet and froze. I could not move up or down. My legs and arms were rigid.

Timothy, standing below to catch me if I fell, called up softly, 'Phill-eep, 'tis no shame to ease your own self back downg to d'san'.'

Slowly I began to back down along the trunk. The bark was rough against my hands and feet, but what I felt most was Timothy's disappointment. I couldn't have been more than a few feet off the ground when I took a deep breath and said to myself, If you fall, you'll fall in sand.

Then I started climbing again.

Timothy called up, 'You 'ave forgot d'knife.'

I knew that if I stopped now, I'd never climb it. I didn't answer him but kept my hands and feet moving steadily. Then I heard him shout, 'You b'gettin' to d'top.' Palm fronds brushed my head. I grasped the base of one to pull myself up. Timothy let out a roar of joy.

Then he told me how to reach the coconuts. It took

a long time to pull, tug, and twist two of them loose. But they finally fell. I stayed in the palm another few minutes to rest, then slid down. I had won.

As my feet touched the ground, Timothy hugged me, yelling, 'D'palm harass us no more.'

We drank every drop of the coconut milk, and feasted on the fresh meat.

Squatting near me, his teeth crunching the coconut, Timothy said, 'You see, Phill-eep, you do not need d'eye now. You 'ave done widout d'eye what I couldn't do wid my whole body.'

It was almost as if I'd graduated from the survival course that Timothy had been putting me through since we had landed on the cay.

It rained that night, a very soft rain. Not even enough to drip through the palm frond roof. Timothy breathed softly beside me. I had now been with him every moment of the day and night for two months, but I had not seen him. I remembered that ugly welted face. But now, in my memory, it did not seem ugly at all. It seemed only kind and strong.

I asked, 'Timothy, are you still black?'

His laughter filled the hut.

CHAPTER 14

One very hot morning in July, we were down on north beach where Timothy had found a patch of calico scallops not too far offshore. It was the hottest day we'd ever had on the cay. So hot that each breath felt like fire. And for once, the trade wind was not blowing. Nothing on the cay seemed to be moving.

North beach was a very strange beach anyway. The sand on it felt coarser to my feet. Everything about it felt different, but that didn't really make sense since it was only about a mile from south beach.

Timothy explained, 'D'nawth is alles d'bleak beach on any islan',' but he couldn't say why.

He had just brought some calico scallops ashore when we heard the rifle shot. He came quickly to my side, saying, 'Dat b'trouble.'

Trouble? I thought it meant someone had found the cay. That wasn't trouble. Excited, I asked, 'Who's shooting?'

'D'sea,' he said.

I laughed at him, 'The sea can't shoot a rifle.'

'A crack like d'rifle,' he said, worry in his voice. 'It can make d'shot all right, all right. It b'tell us a veree bad starm is comin', Phill-eep. A tempis'.'

I couldn't quite believe that. However, there had been, distinctly, a crack like a rifle or pistol shot.

He said anxiously, 'D'waves do it. Somewhar far off, out beyond d'Grenadines, or in dat pesky bight off Honduras, a hurrican' is spawnin', young bahss. I feel it. What we heeard was a wave passin' dis lil' hombug point.'

I heard him sniffing the air as if he could smell the hurricane coming. Without the wind, there was a breathless silence around our cay. The sea, he told me, was smooth as green jelly. But already, the water was getting cloudy. There were no birds in sight. The sky, he said, had a yellowish cast to it.

'Come along, we 'ave much to do. D'calico scallop can wait dey own self till after d'tempis'.'

We went up to our hill.

Now I knew why he had chosen the highest point of land on the cay for our hut. Even so, I thought, the waves might tumble over it.

The first thing Timothy did was to lash our water keg high on a palm trunk. Next he took the remaining rope that we had and tied it securely around the same sturdy tree. 'In case d'tempis' reach dis high, lock your arms ovah d'rope an' hang on, Phill-eep.'

I realized then why he had used our rope sparingly; why he had made my guideline down to east beach from vines instead of rope. Every day, I learned of something new that Timothy had done so we could survive.

During the afternoon, he told me this was a freak storm, because most did not come until September or October. August, sometimes. Seldom in July. 'But dis year, d'sea be angry wid all d'death upon it. D'wahr.'

The storms bred, Timothy said, in the eastern North Atlantic, south of the Cape Verde Islands, in the fall, but sometimes, when they were freaks, and early, they bred much closer, in a triangle way off the northeast tip of South America. Once in a great while, in June or July, they sometimes made up not far from Providencia and San Andrés. Near us. The June ones were only pesky, but the July ones were dangerous.

'Dis be a western starm, I b'guessin'. Dey outrageous strong when dey come,' he said.

Even Stew Cat was nervous. He was around my legs whenever I moved. I asked Timothy what we should do to protect him. He laughed. 'Stew Cat b'go up d'palm on d'lee side iffen it b'gettin' too terrible. Don' worry 'bout Stew Cat.'

Yet I could not help worrying. The thought of

losing either of them was unbearable. If something bad happened on the cay, I wanted it to happen to all of us.

Nothing changed during the afternoon, although it seemed to get even hotter. Timothy spent a lot of time down at the raft, stripping off everything usable and carrying it back up the hill. He said we might never see it again, or else it might wash up the hill so that it would be impossible to launch.

Timothy was not purposely trying to frighten me about the violence of the storm; he was just being honest. He had good reason to be frightened himself.

'In '28, I be on d'*Hettie Redd* sout' o' Antigua when d'tempis' hit. D'wind was outrageous, an' d'ol' schooner break up like chips fallin' 'fore d'axe. I wash ashore from d'sea, so wild no mahn believe it. No odder mahn from d'*Hettie Redd* live 'ceptin' me.'

I knew that wild sea from long ago was much on Timothy's mind all afternoon.

We had a huge meal late in the day, much bigger than usual, because Timothy said we might not be able to eat for several days. We had fish and coconut meat, and we each drank several cups of coconut milk. Timothy said that the fish might not return to the reef for at least a week. He'd noticed that they'd already gone to deep water.

After we ate, Timothy carefully cleaned his knife and put it into the tin box, which he lashed high on the same tree that held our water keg.

'We ready, Phill-eep,' he said.

CHAPTER 15

At sunset, with the air heavy and hot, Timothy described the sky to me. He said it was flaming red and that there were thin veils of high clouds. It was so still over our cay that we could hear nothing but the rustling of the lizards.

Just before dark, Timothy said, ''Twon't be long now, Phill-eep.'

We felt a light breeze that began to ripple the smooth sea. Timothy said he saw an arc of very black clouds to the west. They looked as though they were beginning to join the higher clouds.

I gathered Stew Cat close to me as we waited,

feeling the warm breeze against my face. Now and then, there were gusts of wind that rattled the palm fronds, shaking the little hut.

It was well after dark when the first drops of rain spattered the hut, and with them, the wind turned cool. When it gusted, the rain hit the hut like handfuls of gravel.

Then the wind began to blow steadily, and Timothy went out of the hut to look up at the sky. He shouted, 'Dey boilin' ovah now, Phill-eep. 'Tis hurrican', to be sure.'

We could hear the surf beginning to crash as the wind drove waves before it, and Timothy ducked back inside to stand in the opening of the hut, his big body stretched so that he could hang on to the overhead frame, keeping the hut erect as long as possible.

I felt movement around my legs and feet. Things were slithering. I screamed to Timothy who shouted back, 'B'nothin' but d'lil' lizzard, comin' high groun'.'

Rain was now slashing into the hut, and the wind was reaching a steady howl. The crash of the surf sounded closer; I wondered if it was already beginning to push up towards our hill. The rain was icy, and I was wet, head to foot. I was shivering, but more from the thought of the sea rolling over us than from the sudden cold.

In a moment, there was a splintering sound, and Timothy dropped down beside me, covering my body with his. Our hut had blown away. He shouted, 'Phill-eep, put your 'ead downg.' I rolled over on my stomach, my cheek against the wet sand. Stew Cat burrowed down between us.

There was no sound now except the roar of the storm. Even the sound of the wind was being beaten down by the wildness of the sea. The rain was hitting my back like thousands of hard berries blown from air guns.

Once something solid hit us and then rolled on. 'Sea grape,' Timothy shouted. It was being torn up by the roots.

We stayed flat on the ground for almost two hours, taking the storm's punishment, barely able to breathe in the driving rain. Then Timothy shouted hoarsely, 'To d'palm.'

The sea was beginning to reach for our hilltop, climbing the forty feet with raging whitecaps. Timothy dragged me towards the palm. I held Stew Cat against my chest.

Standing with his back to the storm, Timothy put my arms through the loops of rope, and then roped himself, behind me, to the tree.

Soon, I felt water around my ankles. Then it washed to my knees. It would go back and then crash against us again. Timothy was taking the full blows of the storm, sheltering me with his body. When the water receded, it would tug at us, and Timothy's strength would fight against it. I could feel the steel in his arms as the water tried to suck us away.

Even in front of him, crushed against the trunk of the palm, I could feel the rain, which was now jabbing into me like the punches of a nail. It was not falling towards earth but being driven straight ahead by the wind.

We must have been against the palm for almost an hour when suddenly the wind died down and the rain became gentle. Timothy panted. 'D'eye! We can relax a bit till d'odder side o' d'tempis' hit us.'

I remembered that hurricanes, which are great circling storms, have a calm eye in the centre.

'Are you all right?' I asked.

He replied hoarsely, 'I b'damp, but all right.'

Yet I heard him making small noises, as if it were painful to move, as we stood back from the palm trunk. We sat down on the ground beside it, still being pelted with rain, to wait for the eye to pass. Water several inches deep swirled around us, but was not tugging at us.

It was strange and eerie in the eye of the hurricane. I knew we were surrounded on all sides by violent winds, but the little cay was calm and quiet. I reached over for Timothy. He was cradling his head in his arms, still making those small noises, like a hurt animal.

In twenty or thirty minutes, the wind picked up sharply and Timothy said that we must stand against the palm again. Almost within seconds, the full fury of the storm hit the cay once more. Timothy pressed me tightly against the rough bark.

It was even worse this time, but I do not remember everything that happened. We had been there awhile when a wave that must have reached halfway up the palms crashed against us. The water went way over my head. I choked and struggled. Then another giant wave struck us. I lost consciousness then. Timothy did, too, I think.

When I came to, the wind had died down, coming at us only in gusts. The water was still washing around our ankles, but seemed to be going back into the sea now. Timothy was still behind me, but he felt cold and limp. He was sagging, his head down on my shoulder.

'Timothy, wake up,' I said.

He did not answer.

Using my shoulders, I tried to shake him, but the massive body did not move. I stood very still to see if he was breathing. I could feel his stomach moving and I reached over my shoulder to his mouth. There was air coming out. I knew that he was not dead.

However, Stew Cat was gone.

I worked for a few minutes to release my arms from the loops of rope around the palm trunk, and then slid out from under Timothy's body. He slumped lifelessly against the palm. I felt along the ropes that bound his forearms to the trunk until I found the knots.

With his weight against them, it was hard to pull them loose, even though they were sailor's knots and had loops in them. The rope was soaked, which made it worse.

I must have worked for half an hour before I had him free from the trunk. He fell backwards into the wet sand, and lay there moaning. I knew there was very little I could do for him except to sit by him in the light rain, holding his hand. In my world of darkness, I had learned that holding a hand could be like medicine.

After a long while, he seemed to recover. His first words, painful and dragged out, were, 'Phill-eep . . . you . . . all right . . . be true?'

'I'm okay, Timothy,' I said.

He said weakly, 'Terrible tempis'.'

He must have rolled over on his stomach in the sand, because his hand left mine abruptly. Then he went to sleep, I guess.

I touched his back. It felt warm and sticky. I ran my hand lightly down it, suddenly realizing that I, too, was completely naked. The wind and sea had torn our tatters of clothes from us.

Timothy had been cut to ribbons by the wind, which drove the rain and tiny grains of sand before it. It had flayed his back and his legs until there were very few places that weren't cut. He was bleeding, but there was nothing I could do to stop it. I found his hard, horny hand again, wrapped mine around it, and lay down beside him.

I went to sleep too.

Sometime long after dawn, I awakened. The rain had stopped, and the wind had died down to its usual whisper. But I think the clouds were still covering the sky because I could not feel the sun.

I said, 'Timothy,' but he did not answer me. His hand was cold and stiff in mine.

Old Timothy, of Charlotte Amalie, was dead.

I stayed there beside him for a long time, very tired, thinking that he should have taken me with him wherever he had gone. I did not cry then. There are times when you are beyond tears.

I went back to sleep, and this time when I awakened, I heard a meow. Then I cried for a long time, holding Stew Cat tight. Aside from him, I was blind and alone on a forgotten cay.

CHAPTER 16

*I*n the afternoon, I groped west along the hill. Thirty
or forty feet from the last palm tree, I began to dig
a grave for Timothy. I cleared palm fronds, chunks of
sea grape, pieces of wood, dead fish, fan coral, and
shells that the sea had thrown up. I marked out a space
about seven feet long and four feet wide. Then I dug
with my hands.

At first I was angry with Timothy. I said to Stew
Cat, 'Why did he leave us alone here?' Then as I dug, I
had other thoughts.

With his great back to the storm, taking its full
punishment, he had made it possible for me to live.

When my grandfather died, my father had said, 'Phillip, sometimes people die from just being very, very tired.' I think that is what happened to Timothy.

I also think that had I been able to see, I might not have been able to accept it all. But strangely, the darkness separated me from everything. It was as if my blindness were protecting me from fear.

I buried Timothy, placing stones at the head of the grave to mark it. I didn't know what to say over the grave. I said, 'Thank you, Timothy,' and then turned my face to the sky. I said, 'Take care of him, God, he was good to me.'

There didn't seem to be anything else to say, so I just stood by his grave for a while. Then I felt my way back to the spot where our hut had been. I located wood and piled it around the base of the palm tree that held our water keg and the tin box. Both were to the lee side of the storm.

It took me a long time to get the keg and the tin box to the ground, but I found, on opening the bung, that the water was still sweet and that the matches, wrapped in cellophane inside the tin box, were dry. But the two small bars of chocolate that we had been saving for a 'feast', were ruined. I had no taste for them, anyway.

Feeling it everywhere under my feet, I knew that the cay was littered with debris. I started cleaning the camp area, or what was left of it. I piled all the palm fronds, frayed by the wind, in one place; sticks of wet driftwood in another.

With Stew Cat constantly around – I stumbled over

him several times – I worked until I felt it was nearing
darkness. I'd found one lone coconut in a mass of sea
grape and broken sticks. I opened it and ate the meat,
offering to share with Stew Cat, who didn't seem interested.

Then I made a bed of palm fronds and sprawled out
on it, listening to the still angry sea as it tumbled
around the damp cay and thinking: I must feed myself
and Stew Cat; I must rebuild the hut and build another
signal fire down on east beach; then I must spend each
day listening for the sound of aircraft. I knew Timothy
had already given up on any schooner entering the
dangerous Devil's Mouth.

I was certain that the sea had washed away Timothy's
markers atop the coral reef, and I was also sure that my
guide vine-rope leading down to the beach had been
snapped and tangled by the storm.

But now, for the first time, I fully understood why
Timothy had so carefully trained me to move around
the island, and the reef . . .

The reef, I thought.

How could I fish without any poles? They must
have been washed away. Then I remembered Timothy
saying that he would put them in a safe place. The
trouble was he'd forgotten to tell me where.

I got up and began to run my hands over each palm
trunk. On one of them I touched rope. I followed it
around to the lee side with my fingers. And there they
were! Not two or three, but at least a dozen, lashed
together, each with a barbed hook and bolt sinker.

They were one more part of the legacy Timothy had left me.

The sun came out strong in the morning. I could feel it on my face. It began to dry the island, and towards noon, I heard the first cry of a bird. They were returning.

By now, I had taught myself to tell time, very roughly, simply by turning my head towards the direct warmth of the sun. If the angle was almost overhead, I knew it was around noon. If it was low, then of course, it was early morning or late evening.

There was so much to do that I hardly knew where to start. Get a campfire going, pile new wood for a signal fire, make another rain catchment for the water keg, weave a mat of palm fibres to sleep on. Then make a shelter of some kind, fish the hole on the reef, inspect the palm trees to see if any coconuts were left – I didn't think any could be up there – and search the whole island to discover what the storm had deposited. It was enough work for weeks, and I said to Stew Cat, 'I don't know how we'll get it all done.' But something told me I must stay very busy and not think about myself.

I accomplished a lot in three days, even putting a new edge on Timothy's knife by honing it on coral. I jabbed it into the palm nearest my new shelter, so that I would always know where it was if I needed it. Without Timothy's eyes, I was finding that in my world, everything had to be very precise; an exact place for everything.

On the fifth day after the storm, I began to scour the island to find out what had been cast up. It was exciting, and I knew it would take days or weeks to accomplish. I had made another cane, and beginning with east beach, I felt my way back and forth, reaching down to touch everything that my cane struck; sometimes having to spend a long time trying to decide what it was that I held in my hands.

I found several large cans and used one of them to start the 'time' can again, dropping five pebbles into it so that the reckoning would begin again from the night of the storm. I discovered an old broom, and a small wooden crate that would make a nice stool. I found a piece of canvas, and tried to think of ways to make pants from it, but I had no needle or thread.

Other than that, I found many shells, some bodies of dead birds, pieces of cork, and chunks of sponge, but nothing I could really put to good use.

It was on the sixth day after the storm, when I was exploring on south beach, that I heard the birds. Stew Cat was with me, as usual, and he growled when they first screeched. Their cries were angry, and I guessed that seven or eight might be in the air.

I stood listening to them; wondering what they were. Then I felt a beat of wing past my face, and an angry cry as the bird dived at me. I lashed out at it with my cane, wondering why they were attacking me.

Another dived down, screaming at me, and his bill nipped the side of my head. For a moment, I was confused, not knowing whether to run for cover under sea grape, or what was left of it, or try to fight them off with my cane. There seemed to be a lot of birds.

Then one pecked my forehead sharply, near my eyes, and I felt blood run down my face. I started to walk back towards camp, but had taken no more than three or four steps when I tripped over a log. I fell into the sand, and at the same time, felt a sharp pain in the back of my head. I heard a raging screech as the bird soared up again. Then another bird dived at me.

I heard Stew Cat snarling and felt him leap up on my back, his claws digging into my flesh. There was another wild screech, and Stew Cat left my back, leaping into the air.

His snarls and the wounded screams of the bird filled the stillness over the cay. I could hear them battling in the sand. Then I heard the death caw of the bird.

I lay still a moment. Finally, I crawled to where Stew Cat had his victim. I touched him; his body was rigid and his hair was still on edge. He was growling, low and muted.

Then I touched the bird. It had sounded large, but it was actually rather small. I felt the beak; it was very sharp.

Slowly, Stew Cat began to relax.

Wondering what had caused the birds to attack me, I felt around in the sand. Soon, my hand touched a warm shell. I couldn't blame the birds very much. I'd accidentally walked into their new nesting ground.

They were fighting for survival, after the storm, just as I was. I left Stew Cat to his unexpected meal and made my way slowly back to camp.

CHAPTER 17

Ten pebbles had gone into my 'time' can when I decided to do something Timothy had told me never to do. I was tired of eating fish and sea-grape leaves, and I wanted to save the few green coconuts I'd managed to find on the ground. There were none left in the trees.

I wanted scallops or a langosta to roast over the fire. I didn't dare go out off north beach for scallops because of the sharks. But I thought there might be a langosta clinging to coral at the bottom of the fishing hole.

From what Timothy had told me, the sea entrance to the hole was too narrow for a large fish, a shark, to swim through. Barracuda, he'd said, could go through, but they were not usually dangerous. If there happened to be an octopus down there, it would have to be a very small one. The big ones were always in deep water. So he'd said it was safe for him to dive in the hole.

I sharpened a stick the way Timothy had done, but I knew that if I felt a langosta with my left hand, I would have to be very quick with my right hand, or he would use his tail to push away from me across the sand.

With Stew Cat, I went down to the reef and felt my way along it until I found the familiar edges of the hole. I told Stew Cat, 'If I'm not out in twenty minutes, you better jump in and get me.'

The crazy cat rubbed along my leg and purred.

Holding the sharpened stick in my right hand, I slipped into the warm water, treading for a moment, waiting to see if anything came up. Then I ducked my head underwater, swam down a few feet, and came up again. I was certain that nothing was in the hole aside from the usual small fish I yanked out each morning.

After a few minutes, I had my courage up and dived to the bottom, holding the sharp stick in my left hand now, and using my right hand to feel the coral and rocks. Coming up now and then for air, I slowly felt my way around the bottom of the small pool, touching sea fans that waved back and forth, feeling the organ-pipe coral and the bigger chunks of brain coral.

Several times I was startled when seaweed or sea fans

would brush against my face and swam quickly to the surface. It must have taken me thirty minutes to decide that I could hunt langosta in the hole.

This time, I dived in earnest. I went straight down, touched the bottom, and then took a few strokes towards the coral sides of the pool. Timothy had said that langosta were always on the bottom, usually over against the rocks and coral. To my amazement, I touched one on the first sweep and drove the sharp stick into him, swimming quickly to the surface.

Panting, I shouted to Stew Cat, 'Lobster tonight!'

I swam to the edge, pushed the langosta off the stick, caught my breath again, and dived.

I dived many times without again touching the hard shell that meant langosta. I began sticking my hands deeper into the shelves and over the ledges near the bottom.

I rested a few minutes, then decided I'd make one more dive. I was happy with the lobster that was now on the reef, but it was quite small, barely a meal for Stew Cat and myself.

I dived again, and this time found what seemed to be an opening into a deep hole. Or at least, the hole went far back. There has to be a big lobster in there, I thought. Up I came again, filled my lungs, and dived immediately.

I ran my hand back into the hole, and something grabbed it.

Terrified, I put my feet against the rocks to pull away. The pain was severe. Whatever had my wrist had the strength of Timothy's arms. I jerked hard and whatever it was came out with my arm, its tail smashing against my chest. I kicked and rose to the surface, the thing still on my wrist, its teeth sunk in deep.

I'm sure I screamed as I broke water, flailing towards the edge of the hole. Then the thing let loose, and I made it up over the side and out of the hole.

Pain shooting up my entire arm, I lay panting on the edge of the pool and gingerly began to feel my wrist. It was bleeding, but not badly. But the teeth had sunk in deep.

It wasn't a fish, because the body felt long and narrow. Some time later, I made an informed guess that it had been a large moray eel. Whatever it was, I never got back into the hole again.

CHAPTER 18

There was no day or night that passed when I didn't listen for sounds from the sky. Both my sense of touch and my sense of hearing were beginning to make up for my lack of sight. I separated the sounds and each became different.

I grew to know the different cries of the birds that flew by the cay, even though I had no idea what any of them were. I made up my own names for them according to the sound of their cries. Only the occasional bleat of the gull gave me a picture of that bird, for I had heard and seen them many times around the sea wall in Willemstad.

I knew how the breeze sounded when it crossed the sea grape. It fluttered the small leaves. When it went through the palm fronds the storm hadn't ripped away, it made a flapping noise.

I knew the rustle of the lizards. Some were still on the island after the storm. I could only guess they'd somehow climbed high into the palms. Otherwise, how could they have lived with water lapping over the entire cay?

I even knew when Stew Cat was approaching me. His soft paws on a dried leaf made only a tiny crackle, but I heard it.

One mid-morning in early August, I was on the hill, near the camp, when I heard the far-off drone of an airplane. It was up-wind from me, but the sound was very clear. I reached down to feel Stew Cat. He had heard it too. His body was tense; his head pointed towards the sound.

I dropped to my knees by the fire, feeling around the edges until I grasped the end of a stick. I drew it back. Timothy had taught me to lay the fire sticks like a wheel, so that the fire burned slowly in the centre, but always had a few unburned ends on the outside. I tended the fire a half dozen times each day.

I spit on the stick until I heard a sizzle. Then I knew there was enough fire or charring on it to light off the base of dried palm fronds beneath the signal fire.

I listened again for the drone. Yes, it was still there. Closer now.

I ran down the hill straight to the signal fire, felt

around the palm fronds, and then pushed the stick over them. I blew on it until I heard the crackle of flames. In a few minutes the signal fire was roaring, and I ran to south beach where I would be able to hear the aircraft without hearing the crackling fire.

Standing on south beach, I listened. The plane *was* coming closer!

I yelled towards the sky. 'Here! Down here!'

I decided to run back to east beach to stand near the fire and the new arrangement of rocks that spelled out 'Help'.

Thinking any moment the plane would dive and I would hear the roar of its engines across the cay at low altitude, I stood with Stew Cat a few feet from the sloshing surf. I waited and waited, but there was no thundering sound from the sky. I could hear nothing but the crackling of the fire, the washing sound of the surf.

I ran back to south beach, where I stood very still and listened.

The plane had gone!

Slowly, I returned to east beach and sat down in sea-grape shade. I put my head down on my arms and sobbed, feeling no shame for what I was doing.

There seemed to be no hope of ever leaving the cay, yet I knew I could not always live this way. One day I would become ill or another storm would rage against the island. I could never survive alone.

There had been many bad and lonely days and nights, but none as bad as this.

Stew Cat came up, purring, rubbing along my legs. I held him a long time, wondering why the aircraft had not come down when the pilots saw the smoke.

At last I thought, perhaps they didn't see the smoke. I knew it was going up into the sky, but was it white smoke that might be lost in the blue-white sky, or was it dark and oily smoke that would make a smudge against the blueness? There was no way to tell.

If only there were some oily boards! The kind that drifted around the waters of the Schottegat. But I knew that the wood floating up on the beach consisted mostly of branches or stumps that had been in the water for weeks or months. There was nothing in them to make dark smoke.

I began to think of all the things on the island. Green palm fronds might send off dark smoke, but until they were dried, they were too tough to tear off the trees. The vines on north beach might make dark smoke, but the leaves on them were very small.

The sea grape! I snapped some off, feeling it between my fingers. Yes, there was oil in it. I got up and went over to the fire, tossing a piece in. In a moment, I heard it popping the way hot grease pops when it is dropped into water.

I knew how to do it now.

The smoke would rise from the cay in a fat, black column to lead the planes up the Devil's Mouth. If I heard another aircraft, I'd start a fire and then throw bundles of sea grape into it until I was certain a strong signal was going up from the island.

Timothy hadn't thought about black smoke, I was sure. That was it!

Feeling better now, I walked back up the hill to gather the few palm fronds that were left for a new fire base.

I woke up at dawn on the morning of 20 August 1942, to hear thunder and wondered when the first drops of rain would spatter on the roof of the shelter. I heard Stew Cat, down near my feet, let off a low growl.

I said, 'It's only thunder, Stew Cat. We need the water.'

But as I continued to listen, it did not seem to be thunder. It was a heavy sound, hard and sharp, not rolling. More like an explosion or a series of explosions. It felt as if the cay were shaking. I got up from the mat, moving out from under the shelter.

The air did not feel like rain. It was dry and there was no heavy heat.

'They're explosions, Stew,' I said. 'Very near us.'

Maybe destroyers, I thought. I could not hear any aircraft engines. Maybe destroyers fighting it out with enemy submarines. And those heavy, hard, sharp sounds could be the depth charges that my father said were used by the Navy to sink U-boats.

This time, I didn't bother to take a piece of firewood down to east beach. I dug into the tin box for the cellophane wrapped package of big wooden matches. Four were left. I ran down the hill.

At the signal fire, I searched around for a rock.

Finding one, I knelt down by the fire and struck a match against it. Nothing happened. I felt the head of the match. The sulphur had rubbed off. I struck another. It made a small popping noise and then went out.

I had two more matches left, and for a moment, I didn't know whether to use them or run back up the hill to the campfire.

I stopped to listen, feeling sweat trickle down my face. The explosions were still thundering across the sea.

Then I heard the drone of an aircraft. I took a deep breath and struck the next to last match. I heard it flare and ran my left hand over the top of it. There was heat. It was burning.

I reached deep into the fire pile, holding the match there until it began to burn the tips of my fingers. The fire caught and in a moment was roaring.

I ran across the beach to begin pulling sea grape down. I carried the first bundle to the fire and threw it in. Soon, I could smell it burning. It began to pop and crackle as the flames got to the natural oils in the branches.

By the time I had carried ten or fifteen bundles of sea grape to the fire, tumbling them in, I was sure that a column of black smoke was rising into the sky over the cay.

Suddenly, a deafening roar swept overhead. I knew it was an aircraft crossing the cay not much higher than the palms. I could feel the wind from it.

Forgetting for a moment, I yelled, 'Timothy, they've come.'

The aircraft seemed to be making a sharp turn. It roared across the cay again, seeming even lower this time because the rush of wind from it was hot. I could smell exhaust fumes.

I yelled, 'Down here, down here,' and waved my arms.

The plane made another tight circle, coming back almost directly over me. Its engine was screaming.

I shouted at Stew Cat, 'We'll be rescued!' But I think that he'd gone to hide in the sea grape.

This time, however, the aircraft did not circle back. It did not make another low pass over the island. I heard the sound going away. Soon, it had vanished completely. Then I realized that the explosions had stopped too.

A familiar silence settled over the cay.

All the strength went out of my body. It was the first real chance of rescue, and maybe there would not be another. The pilot had flown away, perhaps thinking I was just another native fisherman waving at an aircraft. I knew that the colour of my skin was very dark now.

Worse, I knew that the smoke might have blotted out the lines of rocks that spelled help.

Feeling very ill, I climbed the slope again, throwing myself down on the mat in the hut. I didn't cry. There was no use in doing that.

I wanted to die.

After a while, I looked over towards Timothy's grave. I said, 'Why didn't you take us with you?'

CHAPTER 19

*I*t was about noon when I heard the bell.

It sounded like bells I'd heard in St Anna Bay and in the Schottegat. Small boats and tugs use them to tell the engineer to go slow or fast or put the engines in reverse.

For a moment, I thought I was dreaming.

Then I heard the bell again. And with it, the slow chugging of an engine. And voices! They were coming from east beach.

I ran down there. Yes, a small boat had come into the Devil's Mouth and was approaching our cay.

I yelled, 'I'm here! I'm here!'

There was a shout from across the water. A man's voice. 'We see you!'

I stood there on east beach, Stew Cat by my feet, looking in the direction of the sounds. I heard the bell again; then the engine went into reverse, the propeller thrashing. Someone yelled, 'Jump, Scotty, the water's shallow.'

The voice was American, I was certain.

The engine was now idling, and someone was coming towards me. I could hear him padding across the sand. I said, 'Hello.'

There was no answer from the man. I suppose he was just staring at me.

Then he yelled to someone on the boat, 'My Lord, it's a naked boy. And a cat!'

The person on the boat yelled, 'Anyone else?'

I called out, 'No, just us.'

I began to move towards the man on the beach.

He gasped. 'Are you blind?'

I said, 'Yes, sir.'

In a funny voice, he asked, 'Are you all right?'

'I'm fine now. You're here,' I said.

He said. 'Here, boy, I'll help you.'

I said, 'If you'll carry Stew Cat, you can just lead me to the boat.'

After I had climbed aboard, I remembered Timothy's knife stuck in the palm tree. It was the only thing I wanted off the cay. The sailor who had carried Stew Cat went up the hill to get it while the other sailor asked me questions. When the first sailor came back from the hill, he said, 'You wouldn't believe what's up there.' I guess he was talking about our hut and the rain catchment. He should have seen the ones Timothy built.

I don't remember everything that happened in the next few hours but very soon I was helped up the gangway of a destroyer. On deck I was asked so many questions all at once that one man barked, 'Stop badgering him. Give him food, medical care, and get him into a bunk.'

A voice answered meekly, 'Yes, sir, Cap'n.'

Down in sick bay, the captain asked, 'What's your name, son?'

'Phillip Enright. My father lives in Willemstad. He works for Royal Dutch Shell,' I answered.

The captain told someone to get a priority radio message off to the naval commander at Willemstad and then asked, 'How did you get on that little island?'

'Timothy and I drifted on to it after the *Hato* was sunk.'

'Where's Timothy?' he asked.

I told the captain about Timothy and what had happened to us. I'm not sure the captain believed any of it, because he said quietly, 'Son, get some sleep. The *Hato* was sunk way back in April.'

I said, 'Yes, sir, that's right,' and then a doctor came in to check me over.

That night, after the ship had been in communication with Willemstad, the captain visited me again to tell me that his destroyer had been hunting a German submarine when the plane had spo ted my black smoke and radioed back to the ship.

There was still disbelief in his voice when he said he'd checked all the charts and publications on the bridge; our cay was so small that the charts wouldn't even dignify it with a name. But Timothy had been right. It was tucked back up in the Devil's Mouth.

The next morning, we docked at the naval base in Cristóbal, Panama, and I was rushed to a hospital, although I really didn't think it was necessary. I was strong and healthy, the doctor on the destroyer had said.

My mother and father flew over from Willemstad in a special plane. It was minutes before they could say anything. They just held me, and I knew my mother was crying. She kept saying, 'Phillip, I'm sorry, I'm so sorry.'

The Navy had notified them that I was blind, so that it would not be a shock. And I knew I looked different. They'd brought a barber in to cut my hair, which had grown quite long.

We talked for a long time, Stew Cat on my bed, and I tried to tell them all about Timothy and the cay. But it was very difficult. They listened, of course, but I had the feeling that neither of them really understood what had happened on our cay.

Four months later, in a hospital in New York, after many X-rays and tests, I had the first of three operations. The piece of timber that had hit me the night the *Hato* went down had damaged some nerves. But after the third operation, when the bandages came off, I could see again. I would always have to wear glasses, but I could see. That was the important thing.

In early April, I returned to Willemstad with my mother, and we took up life where it had been left off the previous April. After I'd been officially reported lost at sea, she'd gone back to Curaçao to be with my father. She had changed in many ways. She had no thoughts of leaving the islands now.

I saw Henrik van Boven occasionally, but it wasn't the same as when we'd played the Dutch or the British. He seemed very young. So I spent a lot of time along St Anna Bay, and at the Ruyterkade market talking to the black people. I liked the sound of their voices. Some of them had known old Timothy from Charlotte Amalie. I felt close to them.

At war's end, we moved away from Scharloo and Curaçao. My father's work was finished.

Since then, I've spent many hours looking at charts of the Caribbean. I've found Roncador, Rosalind, Quito Sueño, and Serranilla Banks; I've found Beacon Cay and North Cay, and the islands of Providencia and San Andrés. I've also found the Devil's Mouth.

Someday, I'll charter a schooner out of Panama and explore the Devil's Mouth. I hope to find the lonely little island where Timothy is buried.

Maybe I won't know it by sight, but when I go ashore and close my eyes, I'll know this was our own cay. I'll walk along east beach and out to the reef. I'll go up the hill to the row of palm trees and stand by his grave.

I'll say, 'Dis b'dat outrageous cay, eh, Timothy?'

AFTERWORD

The dedication at the start of this story is to 'Dr King's dream', and is dated April 1968. It is the key to the whole book, reflecting its author's hopes and aims, and the emotional turmoil of his own country while he was writing it.

Dr Martin Luther King was black. He was an inspiring preacher, the leader of the powerful but non-violent civil rights movement in the United States of America that had sprung up in the 1950s, and winner of the Nobel Peace Prize. On 4 April 1968, he was shot dead on the balcony of a small motel in Memphis, Tennessee. As black people all over America heard the news, their grief, rage and pent-up frustration boiled over in savage riots.

The sixties had seen a second wave of black and white civil rights campaigners, many of them schoolchildren and students, facing what was often a murderous determination to deny blacks respect and equality. Dr King had also publicly opposed the war in Vietnam: 'We have been repeatedly faced with the cruel irony of watching Negro and white boys on TV screens as they kill and die together for a nation that has been unable to seat them together in the same schools.' (The capital N for Negro, which at that time was the courteous word for a black person, was still a recent introduction.)

The Cay

The Cay, then, was published at a time of fierce emotions. But Theodore Taylor chose to set his novel twenty-five or so years earlier, during the Second World War. At that time, official segregation and discrimination against 'coloureds' in the States was total, so that black soldiers were fighting in foreign lands for a freedom they themselves were denied back home. (Martin Luther King used to recall that, in his country's fight for its own freedom, 'the first man to die in the American Revolution was a Negro seaman' – one like Timothy, perhaps.)

To Taylor's readers, the comparison with the sixties was disturbingly clear, but this distant setting allowed his book to be a *story*, a work of art, and not just a moral lecture. It also made the days of actual slavery very close – Timothy's mother and father, like the old lady who had brought him up, would have been slaves.

But here we are, *another* twenty-five years on, and we still need books like this to teach us about respecting each other – something that must have grieved Taylor when he finally decided to write a 'prequel-sequel', *Timothy of the Cay*. This tells the stirring story of Timothy's life before that torpedo attack, cleverly dove-tailed with Phillip's reaction to the world he had come back to. If you've been touched by *The Cay*, you will love it.

But *The Cay* has not won eleven literary awards and sold millions of copies all over the world simply because it has a message! What has made it a classic?

Well, like such other 'classics' as Hemingway's *The*

Afterword

Old Man and the Sea, *The Snow Goose* by Paul Gallico, or *Lord of the Flies* by William Golding, it is short, satisfyingly shaped, and tackles a big theme in simple, direct language – here, through the thoughts of young Phillip.

To be shipwrecked on an island has eternal appeal: there's the struggle to survive, the fascination of ingenious practical details, the hopes and disappointments of being rescued. The isolation of Timothy and Phillip allows a close relationship to develop, and forces them, and us, to explore the idea of dependency, and to ask hard questions. What *is* wisdom? Is it different from cleverness or knowledge?

Phillip's blindness not only adds to the terror of the situation, it puts him – a white child who has inherited his mother's prejudices – entirely at the mercy of the skills, foresight, encouragement and tenderness of old, black, uneducated Timothy. It is also, perhaps, a metaphor, or symbol, for the inability of all prejudiced people to see the truth. Of course, in his own darkness Phillip discovered that Timothy was neither black nor white.

In a way, Phillip's mother is blind too. Brought up in a white country where blacks were treated as outsiders, she found herself a foreigner in a black country. She is homesick and frightened of the war. While she loves Phillip – too much, even – it is an enclosing, restrictive love, not an expansive, giving one. She is unimaginative, unable to see into other people's minds and feelings.

Through his mother, Phillip learned words that have echoed through the centuries all over the world. 'They are not the same as you ... they are different ... That's the way it must be.' But Phillip reveals the pettiness of prejudice in his rage, revulsion and withdrawal, because these are a *child's* feelings. It is always Timothy who puts things into perspective. 'I don' like some white people my own self, but 'twould be outrageous if I didn' like any o' dem.'

Like the black soldiers and seamen, Timothy sacrificed himself to give Phillip life. The important, glorious difference is that by then Phillip loved him.

Stephanie Nettell